FIC
Ange

FIC
ANGE

Angell, Judie

Don't rent my room!

1011

Don't Rent My Room!

Don't Rent My Room!

JUDIE ANGELL

BANTAM BOOKS
NEW YORK • TORONTO • LONDON • SYDNEY • AUCKLAND

DON'T RENT MY ROOM!
A Bantam Book / September 1990

*The Starfire logo is a registered trademark of Bantam Books,
a division of Bantam Doubleday Dell Publishing Group, Inc.
Registered in U.S. Patent and Trademark Office and elsewhere.*

Library of Congress Cataloging-in-Publication Data

Angell, Judie.
   Don't rent my room! / Judie Angell.
     p.   cm.
   Summary: Fifteen-year-old Lucy is apprehensive about leaving the
city for the country when her parents decide to run an inn on the
New England coast.
   ISBN 0-553-07023-1
   [1. Hotels, motels, etc.—Fiction. 2. Family life—Fiction.
3. Country life—Fiction.] I. Title.
   Pz7.A5824D0 1990
[Fic]—dc20   89-18668
                                              CIP

Published simultaneously in the United States and Canada

*Bantam Books are published by Bantam Books, a division of Bantam
Doubleday Dell Publishing Group, Inc. Its trademark, consisting of the
words "Bantam Books" and the portrayal of a rooster, is Registered
in U.S. Patent and Trademark Office and in other countries. Marca
Registrada. Bantam Books, 666 Fifth Avenue, New York, New York 10103.*

PRINTED IN THE UNITED STATES OF AMERICA

BVG   0 9 8 7 6 5 4 3 2

Chapter One

Lucy Weber poked at the plate full of her grandmother's famous mashed potatoes. Ordinarily Lucy shoveled them into her mouth. Now she pushed them around with her fork as she watched her mother argue with her grandmother.

"Pass the butter, please," Sandy, Lucy's mother, said through clenched teeth.

"It's sitting right in front of you," Lucy's grandmother, Martha, answered as she sniffed.

Sandy looked down and exhaled loudly as she stuck her butter knife in and took a pat.

Lucy bit her upper lip.

Except for the sounds of Lucy's two younger brothers slurping their milk, the usually noisy dining room in Lucy's grandmother's large apartment was silent.

"This is just delicious, Martha!" Lucy's father's deep voice sounded just a bit too cheerful.

"Well. Thank you, Red," Martha replied with a nod. "I wonder if your wife is enjoying it as well—"

"It's wonderful, Mother, it's just perfect," Sandy managed as she clicked her tongue and shifted her weight in her chair.

"Thank you."

"You're welcome." Sandy glared at her husband. Pete Weber's hair was actually brown, but Sandy said he had the complexion of a redhead and she'd called him Red since they'd met in college seventeen years ago.

Red smiled and shrugged. "Well, it *is* good," he repeated.

"The least I could do." Martha twisted her napkin in her fingers. "I mean . . . your farewell dinner . . . I just can't *believe* this is the last time we'll all be together this way." She dabbed at her eyes with her napkin.

Sandy threw her linen napkin on the table. "*Moth*-er! This is *not* the last time we'll all be together! I really wish you'd stop this! We're moving to the Cape! A beautiful scenic place. Three hours out of New York City, three hours away from this very apartment building, *door-to-door*! An hour—sixty minutes—on the shuttle! Really, Mother, stop being so dramatic. We'll see each other all the time. Nathan, don't grab."

Nathan put down the two extra soft rolls and dropped one on his plate. At nine he never let arguments interrupt his meals.

"Grandma," Lucy said with a smile, "you know *I* have to see you often. You'll visit and we'll visit you. I'll come back to the city by myself lots of times. I'll take the train or the shuttle. Right, Mom?"

Sandy nodded and scraped her plate with her knife as she cut her chicken.

Lucy's grandma stood up. "Lucy," she said, "come with me into the kitchen. We'll dish out some more potatoes."

"It's okay, there's plenty left in the bowl," thirteen-year-old Henry observed, and promptly scooped some out onto his plate.

"I think we need more," Grandma said, and marched to the swinging doors that led to her small kitchen. After a glance at her parents, Lucy followed.

Once inside the kitchen, Martha clung to her

granddaughter. "Lucy, Lucy, I'm going to miss you so, I can't bear it," she wailed. "And of all the silly, absolutely foolish things to do! Simply chuck every-thing—give up a whole life, a whole *lifestyle*—and go off into the woods, into the *motel* business . . . I still cannot fathom what possessed your parents."

"Grandma, it's not the motel busin—"

"Your mother had a respectable and important position in one of the most well-known brokerage houses on Wall Street!"

Lucy, still holding her grandmother, patted her on the back. "I know, Grandma," she said. "But she—"

"And your *father*! A professor at one of this country's finest universities!"

"Yeah, but they—"

"They have *everything* right here in New York City. They'll be *miserable* out there in no-man's-land. New England! What's there besides snow and beaches?"

Lucy sat her grandmother down at the kitchen table and took her hand.

"Grandma," she said, "I don't like this either. You know I hate it."

"I know, poor darling—"

"I didn't ask for this move. But Mom and Dad . . . I mean, ever since they saw this place and it was for sale, they couldn't talk about anything else! They really love it. They really want this, to own this place and be . . . you know . . ."

"Innkeepers."

"Yeah. Innkeepers."

Martha sighed. "Have you seen it yet?"

"What, the inn? Sure."

"What's it like?"

"They told you." Lucy smiled. "They showed you pictures."

"I didn't pay any attention."

"Yeah, I know. Well, it's old. It's just . . . like a big house, that's all. It's on the ocean—"

"You're going to miss all your friends. And your school," Martha said. "What are you starting now, your sophomore year?"

Lucy nodded. "Tenth grade."

Martha pulled her hands away and wrung them together. "I just can't believe they're up*rooting* you this way! Such a vulnerable age . . . fourteen—"

"Fifteen."

"Fifteen, such a vulnerable age—"

Lucy stood and brushed at her skirt. "Well," she said, "there isn't a lot I can do about it. The apartment's sold, we'll be out of it tomorrow, and I can't exactly commute to my high school in New York from the middle of the Cape in Massachusetts. Besides, nothing can rain on Mom and Dad's parade, they're so excited. Let's just get the potatoes and bring them out to Henry and Daddy, who'll just—" She looked at her grandmother's face. "Grandma? What is it?"

Martha stood suddenly and clapped her hands together. "Lucy!" she cried.

"What?"

"You'll stay here!"

"What?"

"*Why* didn't I think of this before? You'll stay *here*! With me! In New York! There's plenty of room. You'll be able to continue at school. Everything will work out perfectly! Sandy and Red can go move to their silly inn; you'll stay right here! The boys can visit on vacations and see their friends, too!" Her face was glowing.

Lucy felt a fluttering in the pit of her stomach. "I don't think Mom'll go for it," she said.

"Of course she will!"

Lucy was about to respond when she felt herself being dragged by the wrist through the swinging doors and back into her grandmother's dining room.

"Sandy! Red!" Martha announced. "I have a wonderful idea! And I won't take no for an answer. Lucy will stay right here in New York with me! I'll send her to you on school vacations. And you can send Nathan and Henry back here. It's all settled. Aren't I smart?! Nathan, would you like some more rolls, dear?"

"We're leaving, Mother," Sandy said, standing as she held her jacket and tapped her foot.

"You're not leaving. Stay here and discuss this," Martha said.

"There's nothing to discuss. Come on, Red. Where are the boys?"

"At the elevator."

"Let's go, then. Lucy, don't forget your purse."

"Red, be reasonable," Martha appealed to him. "At least talk it over. Lucy wants to stay!"

"Martha, you're a very dear lady, a lovely mother-in-law, and a terrific cook, but this is overstepping your bounds," Red said. "We're a family, and a family stays together."

"*I'm* family, too!" Martha wailed.

"Yes, you are, Martha, and we want to see you often, but *these* parents want their own children with them."

"Daddy, I thought it was a good idea," Lucy said, trying to sound reasonable and mature.

"You are coming with us, young lady, and I will hear no more about it," Sandy said firmly, and opened the apartment door. "We are leaving, Mother. How could you do this to me!"

Martha looked at her daughter, then leaned out

into the hall. "Boys!" she called. "Nathan, Henry!
Dessert! Chocolate cake—I baked it myself!"

They stampeded back into the apartment. Sandy
and Red followed.

"That was a dirty trick, Mother," Sandy said,
tapping her fingernails on the table.

"Good cake, Grandma," Nathan mumbled, his
mouth full.

"*Great* cake," Henry echoed.

"All right," Martha said, as she reached for Lucy's
hand. "Look here. I need Lucy and she needs me."

"She's not staying here, Mother, and that's final," Sandy said, and tightened her lips.

"Wait a minute," Lucy said, "just wait a minute!
You're all talking about me as if I weren't *here*! I *am*
here! I think I ought to have something to say about
my life!" She paused, waiting for the adults to interrupt her. When no one did, she swallowed hard and
tried quickly to gather her thoughts regarding what
she had to say about her life.

"Um." She cleared her throat. "I don't think it's
fair," she began, "that just because I'm a kid I have
to change my whole life to live your dream." She
looked briefly at her mother, then dropped her head.
"I mean, it's *yours*, not mine, right? But I'm a person too, and it seems like I don't have any rights
just because I'm young, and just because . . . just
because—"

"Just because you don't run a household and
pay the bills," her mother finished. "Well, that's
true. But Lucy, your rights are less equal when your
individual input is not the same as ours. And we
are considering you. You're not exactly being thrown
out on the street."

Red sank into his chair at the table and picked

up his fork to wave as he made his point. "Right!" he said. "One of the main reasons for buying the Scottwood Inn and moving was so that we'd all be living and working in the same place for a change—to bring the family closer together. We hardly ever saw each other, between work and commuting and meetings and seminars and extra hours—"

"Can I have another piece of cake, Grandma?" Nathan asked, obviously not listening to his father.

"I have an idea," Lucy said. "What if I move to the inn with you now and spend the summer," she began.

"Hey, look at that piece he cut!" Henry cried, and made a grab for the cake.

"Boys," Sandy said.

"Is someone going to listen to me or not?" Lucy cried, stamping her foot.

The room was silent. Nathan stopped in mid-chew.

"I mean, maybe we're not exactly in a democracy, but at least you could *listen*." She folded her arms and glared at her parents.

"Okay," her father said.

"Okay, sorry," Sandy said.

"Yeah," Nathan said.

"Not you, you're a kid, you don't count either," Lucy told him.

Her mother turned to her. "Now *you're* not being fair," she said. "We apologized for not listening. Listening is something we should always do, all of us. Go on, Lucy."

Lucy went on glaring at them. She felt guilty after the apology but she wasn't ready to be mollified. "Okay," she said. "Summer vacation is two and a half months. That's a pretty long time. And when Labor Day comes, if I don't like being there, then I'll come back and spend the school year with Grandma. The boys don't care about moving, but I do."

"That sounds like a wonderful compromise!" Martha cried.

"Let go the knife!"

"*You* let go the knife!"

"*Both* of you let go of the knife!" Sandy looked at her sons and then at her husband. Red looked back.

"I don't know about that," Sandy said.

"It's perfectly fair—" Lucy began.

"Yes, but is it fair to us?" her mother interrupted. "We want our family together."

"Well, but do you want everyone together if everyone isn't happy?" Martha said.

"Mother, stay out of this, please. I thought I made myself clear, Lucy. You don't get an equal vote, it's as simple as that."

Lucy made an exasperated noise through her nostrils.

"Look, Lucy," her father said placatingly, "I think it's silly to discuss this now. Really. Because I know that once we all get there, you're going to love it. Of course you're nervous now, not knowing what it's going to be like, not having any friends yet. But honey, all that will take care of itself. I know you'll be happy. I just know it." He grinned his that-should-end-it grin.

"Then if you're so sure, give me the option," Lucy said.

"Aw—"

"No, I mean it. I know I have to do what you say most of the time because I'm a kid, but this is one time we both have a chance to get what we want. I have Grandma to come home to if I'm not happy in"—she made a face—"the *country*."

"No," Sandy said. "No, I won't agree to it because you've already got a mind-set on it."

"I don't."

"Yes, you do. Just the way you said 'the *country*' —as if it were the Siberian isolation ward!"

"I'll be fair! I'll keep an open mind."

"That's easier said than done, Lucy."

Sensing victory, Lucy let her face relax. "I'll give it every chance. I *promise!*"

"You know . . . it's so beautiful," Sandy said almost to herself. "So peaceful. Lucy, you can see the ocean from your bedroom window. . . ." She looked up. "What do you see from your bedroom window here?"

"A red-and-purple-haired woman feeding a canary."

"My point is made."

"Well, they're *both* interesting!"

"I'm not sure about this."

"Lucy," Red said, "we don't want you to be unhappy."

"Thanks."

"But I don't think you will be. Look . . . Sandy . . . let's let her have the option."

"Red—"

"If she spends two and a half months, we all ought to know by then where she stands. If she's miserable, I don't think anyone will be happy if she stays."

"Thanks, Mother," Sandy muttered at Martha, whose eyelashes fluttered.

"Sandy, he's right. You do have the final say, but you don't want Lucy to be unhappy." Lucy's grandmother smiled at her. "And for that reason you're all lucky I'm here!"

"Lucy," her mother said, leaning forward, "you have to promise to give it every chance."

"I *did* promise!"

"*Every* chance."

Sandy stood and spoke as she moved toward

the door. "Good night, Mother. The inn is a wonderful place and I know Lucy will want to stay. We'll call you from the Cape and thanks a lot—for dinner."

"Yes, thanks, Martha." Red tipped an imaginary hat.

"Thank you, Grandma," Henry and Nathan sang.

Lucy and her grandmother hugged each other and cried.

Chapter Two

Lucy sat at her desk, trying to compose a letter to Ruthie, her best friend. *There's a room here,* she wrote, *that the Scottwoods told us George Washington slept in. But my dad says that if George Washington slept in every inn and boardinghouse that claims he did, he would've had to've lived for 300 years! Anyway, the permanent guest here, Mr. Ainsley, says that it wasn't George but a famous general in his army. He told me the name, but I can't remember. It's funny because Mr. Ainsley can't seem to remember my name. Anyway, if you're into history, I guess you'd find it here.* She stopped and tried to decide what impression she wanted to leave with this letter. Was she happy? How happy?

It's pretty, she wrote. *I can't say it's not pretty.*

Her desk faced a window from which she could watch the ocean—calm today, with softly rolling white-capped waves. She watched them until she heard three short raps against her door and recognized her mother's knock. "Come on in, Mom!" she called.

"Hi-i," Sandy sang. She stepped into the room and closed the door softly behind her. "I just can't get used to not *yelling* when I want you! Now I have to run up a flight of stairs."

"Uh-*huh*!" Lucy smirked. "Easier in an apartment, huh?"

"Enough of that. I need you downstairs. Your father's hanging his fishing pictures in the front hall."

"Does he need me to help him?"

"Well, sort of. Mrs. Thatch is standing over him. She keeps telling him they're crooked and that all the pictures show freshwater fish which are from lakes, not oceans, and your father doesn't want to complain to her so he complains to me. Do you think you could divert Mrs. Thatch for a while? She seems to like you. In fact, you're the *only* one she seems to like. What're you doing there?"

Lucy sighed and stood. "Just writing a letter to Ruthie."

"How do you know where to send it?" Sandy asked. Ruthie was on a bike trip to Canada.

"She sent me her intinerary. She's supposed to be in Albany day after tomorrow."

"Now, Lucy, you're not sighing, are you? Did I hear a sigh?"

Lucy laughed. "*No*, Mom, you did not hear a sigh. I understand, really."

"Because we just didn't have the money to send you to all those places your friends are going to this summer—"

"Mom. I know. I'm not complaining. Really!"

"And you know we wanted you with us, because—"

"Aaaaaaagh!"

"All right, all right. Listen, Nathan went down near the water and I'm afraid he's going to drown if someone doesn't tell him to make sure to stay on the lawn. Henry's supposed to be checking the bread and rolls; they're bringing them in from the truck out back. I have to stay at the desk, so if you'd just see to these things—"

"—I'll find a bonus in my pay envelope mid-month."

"Right." Her mother smiled. They went to the door together.

"Hi, Daddy. Hi, Mrs. Thatch." Lucy smiled brightly at their two scowling faces. "Pictures look nice," she added.

"Thanks," Red said, and managed a smile. "Oh, Luce, come with me a minute, there's something I'd like to talk to you about." He took his daughter's elbow and maneuvered her down the hall as Mrs. Thatch, wire-haired and stern-looking, watched them with her arms folded across her ample bosom.

"Luce, she's driving me nuts."

"I know. Mom told me."

"She's the housekeeper. She's supposed to be supervising the help, not the owner," her father complained.

"I'll ask her to call again about the new maid."

"I don't remember her ever even making an appearance when the Scottwoods owned this place."

"I'll divert her. Mom already talked to me about it."

"Good, okay. Hey, Luce?"

"What?"

"How do you like it so far?" He grinned at her.

Lucy stuck her tongue out at him and walked back toward the rigid Mrs. Thatch. "Hi again," she said.

" 'Morning," Mrs. Thatch said. Her arms were still folded. "Like those pictures, do you?"

"Yeah. Dad likes lake fishing. He grew up in Michigan . . . lots of lakes. . . ."

"You were the only one made your own bed today, you know that?" Mrs. Thatch said.

"Oh . . . well . . ."

"Scottwoods all made their own beds. Well, not

all, but I don't count a couple of them. Children should make their own beds. Parents, too."

"Yes, well, maybe they don't mind if their beds aren't made," Lucy said. "Doesn't mean that you or the maids should do it."

"Well, I think—"

"Mrs. Thatch, do you think you could call the agency again? About the new maid? Would you mind?"

"They'll send someone, don't you worry."

"Mom would sure appreciate it if you'd check, okay? Because you're the one who really knows everyone around here."

Mrs. Thatch sniffed. "Well," she said.

"Thanks a million." Lucy was already moving toward the end of the hallway toward the kitchen. "See you later!" she called.

There was a young boy about Henry's age and an older man unloading fresh-smelling wrapped baked goods from a green truck when Lucy arrived at the inn's back pantry. Her brother was checking off items from a long list.

"Henry? You making sure everything's here?" she asked.

Henry gave her a sidelong look. "No, I'm writing jokes for my stand-up routine," he said.

"Cute," Lucy said. "Mom wanted to make sure everything was okay."

"Everything's okay," Henry said.

"Fine."

"Fine."

"Brothers!"

"Sisters!"

Lucy rolled her eyes at the ceiling and left by the back door.

The delivery boy put down an armload of French bread and looked up at Henry. "You live here?" he asked.

"Uh-huh."

"You the new owners?"

"Uh-huh," Henry repeated.

"Yeah, well, good," the boy said. "The folks here before had no young kids around. How old are you?"

"Thirteen."

"Yeah, me too. That your sister who was just here?"

"Yeah."

The boy craned his neck to watch Lucy squeezing past his father's truck as she headed toward the shoreline. "How old is she?"

"Fifteen. Why?"

The boy just shrugged.

"Donald! Quit yakkin'! Let's go!"

The boy glanced toward the side door. "Okay! Listen, I'll see ya," he said to Henry. "Maybe you could come down to the pier. We could go fishin', hang out." This last was spoken as he climbed into the truck. His father took off so fast, Henry didn't have time to answer.

Nathan assured Lucy that he was perfectly fine. This morning, he explained, he planned to skim rocks off the waves and he had absolutely no intention of swimming, much less drowning. He called to her attention the fact that he wasn't even wearing a bathing suit. "I'm nine years old and I don't need a babysitter!"

Lucy turned and stomped back toward the inn. Her brothers were again being nasty to her, both of them in the space of five minutes, she thought as she looked up at the big house.

"You sure can see a lot of sky," she said to herself. About as far from New York as you can get, except maybe . . . the desert.

Mr. Ainsley was rocking on the back porch as Lucy climbed the wooden steps. He was the inn's only permanent guest. Since their arrival a few days ago, he spent his days rocking either on the wide front porch or the back, depending on his mood. Her father said Mr. Ainsley spent his winter days rocking in front of the fire in the big living room. He was so old, her father said, he probably came with the house.

"Hello, Mr. Ainsley!" Lucy spoke right into his face because she knew he was hard of hearing.

Mr. Ainsley's head jerked upward. "OH! HELLO, SUSAN!"

Lucy sighed. "It's Lucy!" she corrected. "Would you like a blanket or something?"

"WATCHING YOUNG HOWARD THROW STONES!" Mr. Ainsley told her, and grinned widely.

"Okay," Lucy said, and walked past him into the house, shaking her head. He calls me "Susan" and Nathan "Howard," the names of the Scott-wood children, she thought. He doesn't call Henry anything at all because there were only two Scott-woods.

She headed for the stairs leading to the family's second-floor quarters. Honestly, Susan Scottwood is probably fifty years old by now!

Think I'll give Grandma a call, she decided, and took the stairs two at a time. But Grandma wasn't home. Lucy left a short, cheery message on her answering machine.

The family and Mrs. Thatch ate their meals at the big old oak table in the kitchen, while the guests dined leisurely in the high-ceilinged dining room next door.

"The Scottwoods always got served in the dining room," Mrs. Thatch had grumbled at first. "It's only fittin', them being the owners, they get served like guests."

"I know, but it feels more like home to me if I help myself in the kitchen," Sandy explained. "I want you to feel at home with our family, too, so why don't you eat with us?"

That mollified the stout Mrs. Thatch, who had never before been invited to have so much as a cup of coffee with the previous owners, except at Christmastime and the annual staff eggnog party.

Together they sat with bowed heads while Nathan said grace. The prayer was a new addition. In the city they had never had time for grace before meals, but Mrs. Thatch had been horrified when everyone dug in haphazardly. As a result, they now took the time to thank the Lord for their daily bread.

". . . and thanks for the mashed potatoes, even though they're not as good as Grandma's, amen," Nathan finished. He quickly passed the mashed potatoes to his father on his left.

"There's a fella coming up here in a couple of days to check out the place for a possible family reunion at the end of the month," Red said. "Called about four."

"Really?" Sandy stopped serving herself.

"Uh-huh. Said about twenty-five people . . . little kids and all—"

"We only have fifteen rooms! And Mr. Ainsley's in one of them."

"I know, I know, calm down." Red pulled apart a roll. "They don't mind bunking up together—that's what a reunion's all about, he said. It seems he and his younger sister remember this place from their childhood or something."

"No kidding?" Henry said. "How old are they now?"

"In their seventies," Red answered, and bit into a drumstick.

"Their seventies! Wow!" Henry whistled. "This place really *is* old!"

"Seventy is not that old, young man," Mrs. Thatch said huffily.

"Maybe they'll all know Mr. Ainsley," Nathan suggested.

"They're babies compared to Mr. Ainsley," Red said with a grin. "He's nearing a hundred!"

Henry glanced sidelong at Mrs. Thatch. "That old enough for you?" he asked.

"Henry!" Sandy said, pursing her lips.

Red looked over at Lucy, who was staring into space.

"Hey, Lucy," he said. "What's up?"

Lucy blinked. "Oh. Just thinking," she said.

"We're all going to have to pitch in tomorrow," her father told her. "Get the place in tip-top condition for that man coming about the reunion. We need the business."

Lucy sighed.

"Lucy?"

"I know, I know," she said. "Just reminds me of when we were selling the apartment. It always had to be so clean every single day. I couldn't wait until that was over! And now—"

"And now we have to do it all the time!" her mother finished.

"I'm calling around again tomorrow for a maid," Mrs. Thatch said. "The first young lady canceled out as a maid. We'll be able to find someone else, though."

Suddenly there was a loud clatter behind them. Everyone jumped.

"Sor-ry," a young waitress said. "It just slipped out of my hands."

Sandy closed her eyes.

"It's okay," Red said with a tight smile.

Chapter Three

Nathan hugged his Bentley-the-Bear and curled up tight inside his goose-down bag as he stared through the screen at the silver-speckled sky. When they'd first seen the three-story white clapboard house with black shutters—real ones that closed over the windows for protection against the weather—he'd loved it as much as his parents did. It had wide porches front and back, with big wide columns, too big for Henry to wrap his arms all the way around. The back porch overlooked a wide expanse of green lawn that led directly to the ocean, and its columns supported still another porch off the second floor. This one was screened in, and it was a wonderful place to bring a sleeping bag for the night if you happened to be a nine-year-old boy and didn't care that the wooden floor was hard and cold and smelled a little of waxed-over mildew.

Nathan listened to the ocean and thought about how lucky he was: lucky that Henry hadn't heard him slip out of their room to come to the screen-porch by himself; lucky that he hadn't met Mr. Ainsley in the hall on his way to the bathroom, as he did nearly every time he came out of his room at night; lucky that it was a perfect night, not too cold from the ocean spray and breezes; and most of all, lucky that he had been born to this mom and dad, who had the good sense to buy this terrific house with so many rooms and people and places to hide and to explore and with the Atlantic Ocean right out there just for him to listen to each night as he fell asleep. He closed his eyes. Why didn't Grandma think this was the best idea in the whole world? Why did his sister Lucy want to go back to the city, where a kid couldn't even run three steps without bumping into something or someone?

Nathan felt a little tug at the foot of his sleeping bag. He shut his eyes tighter and gritted his teeth. Darn! Henry had awakened and found him here, and now he'd have to share his night on the porch with his brother, who talked too much and snored, too.

But no one talked.

Nathan opened his eyes and peered over the lip of his sleeping bag. The little screen-porch was lit by the stars and Nathan had no trouble seeing. There was no one there.

He sighed with relief and rested his head again on his arm. Should have brought my pillow, he thought dreamily. He began to drift off with his head full of stars and ocean.

"Boy!" A voice whispered in his ear.

Nathan sat up quickly. There was no one there.

"Who said that?" Nathan hissed into the dark. But there was no answer.

"Who said 'Boy'?" Nathan repeated. "Come on, Henry. If it's you—"

Nothing.

Nathan clutched at the bag and the bear with both fists and frowned as he looked around.

"Lucy? Is that you?"

He lay back again but he kept his eyes open, darting glances from right to left.

"*Boy!*" he heard again, distinctly and from above him to his left.

But he saw nothing.

Nathan licked his lips. He felt his eyes watering. Still inside the bag, he inched his way to the screen door that led to the main corridor. It took him a while because he couldn't use his hands or his legs, but he made it at last. He leapt out of the bag, leaving it on the floor, and, breathing hard and fast, careened down the hall toward the family's wing.

Lucy hadn't wanted to make her bed the next morning, but she did it because Mrs. Thatch had made such a big deal of the fact that she'd done it before. The Weber household had never cared much about bed-making—if you felt like it, you did it, except for linen-changing days—but here at the inn, where maids and housekeepers wandered in and out, you had to watch your personal habits more carefully.

So because she had slept a little later and was now tugging at sheets and comforters, Lucy was the only one in the family quarters when the telephone rang. She ran for it.

"Hello?"

"Darling! It's Grandma!"

"Grandma! How come you didn't call back yesterday?"

"Sweetheart, I'm so sorry! I just got back here this morning. I was out in Queens, staying with your Cousin Joan."

"My Cousin Joan?"

"Your mother's cousin. You know—what do you call her, Aunt Joan? She's your cousin once removed. Or is she your second cousin? I can never keep these things straight—"

"Right. Joan from Queens. I remember. It's just

been a long time since I've seen her. Christmas, I guess it was. How is she?"

"How is she? Well, that's another story. Meanwhile, tell me how *you* are."

"Well . . ."

"Come on, it's Grandma. Tell me everything!"

"Well—" Lucy giggled, "the housekeeper makes us say grace—"

"No!"

"Yes! And there's an old man here, about a hundred, and he keeps calling me 'Susan' and calls Nathan 'Howard' because those are the names of the children of the people who used to own this place, only they're all grown up now—"

"Oh, Lord!"

"And I really called you yesterday because I don't think Mr. Ainsley has any grandchildren of his own and I . . . just missed you. Anyway, I wanted to make sure you didn't forget my name."

Martha giggled and squealed into the phone. "Aren't you the sweetest thing! Of course I remember your name, Ellen, now tell me more!"

They laughed about the chef, who hung his homemade noodles all over the kitchen; about the waitress who had quit; about the smallness of the village; about the out-of-date movie playing at the only movie house within ten miles.

"Oh, dear!" Grandma cried. "That's enough, my eyes are tearing! Now, really—I want you to tell me exactly how you feel. How is it really? Is it awful?"

Lucy frowned. Awful? Well, it wasn't New York City, it wasn't what she was used to. She missed her friends and the city's bustle, she *knew* that.

She missed her grandma more than anything, but she felt some loyalty to her parents, who were trying so hard. As she laughed about all the little disasters she felt a little guilty.

"Well, no," she said at last. "It's not awful. You know, I *did* make a promise, Grandma. I said I'd keep an open mind."

"I know, of course you did. That's my girl. Now, about your Cousin Joan."

"What about Cousin Joan?"

Chapter Four

"Oh, no!" Sandy cried.

"Oh, yes. Grandma said she'd call you tonight and give you more details. She just wanted you to be prepared."

"I can't believe it. Well, maybe I can. I mean, Joan isn't exactly—I mean, she isn't one you'd always—"

"No," Lucy said, "I hardly remembered her when Grandma said she was out there visiting."

"Very mousy, never opened her mouth. I mean, never! Can't remember Joan ever expressing herself. Ever having an *opinion*!"

"Well, I bet she's got one now."

"Mmmm. The man just walked *out* on her? Never said a *word*?"

"No, I told you. He left a note. 'Dear Joan, Sorry about this, have to follow my heart. Good luck, Harry.' "

"Harry," Sandy repeated. "How long were they married, anyway? Ten years? And he left her for a cosmetology student?"

Lucy nodded. "Twenty-one years old. That's what Grandma said Joan told her."

"So Grandma suggested that Joan come here."

"She says you should give her a job."

"Your grandma has absolutely no idea what we're doing here at all! No idea how a business is run, just 'give her a job!' " Sandy gnashed her teeth.

Lucy shrugged. "Well, now we need a waitress *and* a maid," she suggested.

"Joan couldn't handle either of those jobs." Sandy sighed. "I think she taught aerobics at some health club in Queens. Maybe we could use that. Maybe she wouldn't mind working for room and board. . . ."

"Grandma says she thinks Joan is having a nervous breakdown," Lucy added.

"Me too," her mother said, and sighed.

"Ma! I'm going down to the pier!" Henry yelled from the door.

"Did you help Dad sweep out the bar and polish the floor?" Sandy asked.

"Yeah."

"Are you sure?"

"I'm *sure!*"

"All right—be home by supper. Take Nathan with you!"

Henry rolled his eyes and slammed the screen door. Looking extremely put-upon, he rushed back across the small lobby toward the big staircase. On his way he nearly knocked Red down as he was coming out of the bar.

"Whoa, son! What's the rush?" Red asked.

Henry shuffled his feet. "Aw, Dad—I was just going down to the pier and Mom says I have to take Na-than with me."

"Well, is that so bad?"

"Naw, it's just that I'm hanging out with kids my own age and I don't always want him . . . you know . . ."

Red patted his son on the shoulder. "I know.

But Nathan's been behaving strangely lately. Have you noticed?"

Henry, who hadn't, just shrugged.

"Well, it would be nice if you'd take him with you every now and then. Just until he makes friends of his own. You've been spending a lot of time down at the pier lately, haven't you?"

"Yeah. There's this kid, Donald. His father works for the bakery that delivers bread here. He's been teaching me how to fish."

"Great! Did you read that pamphlet I gave you about the history of the pier?"

Henry nodded. "Yeah," he said, "I did. That boat shed down at the end of the dock? They said that was the most painted structure in the whole country!"

Red grinned. "Right. Because it's such a typical New England sight, I guess. Artists are all over the place down there, aren't they?"

"Yeah. I told Donald about it. He grew up here and he didn't even know that."

"Well, if you're interested, I've got some material about scrimshaw we could look at tonight, maybe," Red suggested.

"Yeah, okay," Henry said, then slapped his father five and went to find his brother.

"He likes history," Red said, smiling at Sandy, who was making notes in the margin of the inn's registry.

"Mm-hm," she said, "he likes to read. Gets it from his dad." She looked up. "But tonight's your night tending bar, remember? Bob's off."

"Oh. Yeah, that's right."

"So much for togetherness at the Scottwood Family Inn." She sighed. "At least for tonight. Starting tomorrow, we'll have even more togetherness than we planned."

"Cousin Joan arrives tomorrow," Red said.

"Cousin Joan arrives tomorrow," his wife echoed.

"I wonder," Red said, "if Harry's new girlfriend looks anything like Honey!" He waggled his eyebrows up and down and Sandy threw her pencil at him.

Honey was the inn's new waitress. She attracted stares throughout the dining room. Honey had black hair, piled high on her small head. She wore layers of makeup and false eyelashes that seemed to precede her into a room. She also arrived for work in a pair of four-inch heels, which she exchanged for black rubber cleats when she waited on tables. She was, however, a good waitress and she seemed reliable, so Red and Sandy decided to overlook the fact that the male guests gawked at her.

"At least," Red said, "you *remember* Honey. I can't remember what Joan looks like when she's left the room for a minute."

"I know," Sandy said. "Maybe that was the problem."

"What room do you want me to give her?" Red asked. "I think she ought to be near us, at least for a while. What do you think?"

"I think you're right. Put her next door in Fourteen."

Nathan Weber kicked open the screen door and stepped out onto the front porch, blinking at the sun. To his right, Mr. Ainsley sat in the wooden rocker, heavily padded with cushions, sipping a glass of pink lemonade Lucy had brought out to him. He scratched his pale freckled head and peered over at Nathan.

"HELLO, HOWARD!" Mr. Ainsley called.

"Hello," Nathan answered.

"HOTTER TODAY, INNIT?"

"Uh-huh."

Mr. Ainsley resumed his rocking and Nathan wandered over to him.

"Mr. Ainsley?"

"EH?"

"You always call me 'Howard.' Is Howard's last name Scottwood?"

"HOWARD? SCOTTWOOD? WHAT'S THE MATTER, HOWARD?"

"Nothing . . . nothing, Mr. Ainsley." Nathan walked down the steps to the sidewalk and headed downtown.

Lucy spent most of the afternoon under the watchful eye of Mrs. Thatch, vacuuming the carpets on the second floor. At around three-thirty, Red came bounding up the stairs followed by a pleasant-faced middle-aged woman in white bib overalls.

"Ladies," he said, "I'd like you to meet Mrs. Overton, our new maid. We just came straight from Crane's Employment Service over on Main Street."

"Hello," Mrs. Overton said, and stuck out her hand. Lucy shook it firmly.

"Boy, am I glad to see you!" she cried.

"Well, me too," Mrs. Overton said. "I'd been working over at the Howard Johnson's at the other end of the Cape, but I wanted a place closer to home. I can walk here." She looked around. "And it's such a pretty old place, isn't it?"

"Now Mrs. Thatch will show Mrs. Overton the routine and you can go out and have some fun," Red said to his daughter.

Mrs. Thatch glowered. "Right there in Eleven,"

Mrs. Thatch said, pointing to the nearest door. "Bath-room needs doing."

"I'll get right on it!" Mrs. Overton sang, and disappeared into Room Eleven.

Mrs. Thatch shook her head. "This inn was built by Scottwoods and Scottwoods have lived in it and run it for four generations. Aren't you training your children to take over?"

Red tucked his hair behind his ears. "Now, Mrs. Thatch," he said, "I know you were upset when we bought the Scottwood, but—"

"No, no, Mr. Weber!" She held up her pudgy hands. "I wasn't the least upset with you folks. I was upset with the ungrateful children. Susan and that no-good brother of hers, Howard. Leaving a priceless legacy to be bought by strangers! Why, old Mercer Scottwood must be spinning over in his grave!" She glanced up at the spot where the original Scottwood's portrait had hung. It had been replaced by a fisherman grasping the lip of a largemouth bass, but his son's and grandson's pictures were still there. They were both glower-ing and looked exactly alike. Mrs. Thatch shook her head. "And all the Mercers who followed him, too. Mercer Junior, and Mercer the Third . . ."

She was still muttering as Red gave his daugh-ter's shoulders a squeeze. "You run along, Luce," he said, "and enjoy the rest of the day. It's pretty out there. Maybe you'll get to meet some of the girls your own age down at The Neck."

"The Neck" was a part of one of the piers where there were shops and boutiques which sold sea art—scrimshaw and paintings and crafts, as well as cloth-ing and souvenirs.

"I've met some people," Lucy said, "but they're all working in the shops. Maybe I'll just go down there and see if I can buy myself a T-shirt for some exorbitant price."

"Maybe you ought to just stay here and vac-uum," her father said with a laugh.

Lucy wasn't looking for her brothers, but she saw them scurrying along the main street of town. Henry was sharing a large box of popcorn with an-other boy Lucy didn't recognize, and Nathan was tagging along behind them.

"Hi!" she called, but they didn't hear her. Na-than was tugging at Henry's shirttail and Henry was ignoring him. The usual, Lucy thought.

She stopped in at a store that sold swimwear and began to admire some of the bathing suits.

"Nice, huh?" said a girl at her elbow. Lucy had met her before, right in this shop. Her name was Caroline Wright and she was sixteen.

"Yeah, they're nice," Lucy agreed, "but they're a bit pricey."

"Mmmm, I know," Caroline said sympathetically. "But wait till the end of the summer and they all go on sale at a fantastic price."

"Uh-huh, but at the end of the summer I won't need them anymore, and by next summer they'll be out of style!"

"You're right." Caroline sighed. "So what do you do?"

"You wear your suit from last year, which is out of style anyway."

Caroline laughed. "So," she said, "how are things going up at the Scottwood?"

"A little hectic, but okay, I guess. My parents are learning"—she shrugged—"how to run an inn. They seem to like it, though."

"Do you?"

"I don't know yet," Lucy answered truthfully.

"You will," Caroline said as she straightened a counter display. "And it's really nice to have a new family around. The Scottwoods were pretty old—they just stayed around the inn all the time, rocking with Mr. Ainsley. Every town needs new blood. Kids grow up and leave, and if new families don't come in, the town dies."

Lucy longingly touched the shocking pink fabric of a maillot suit. "I guess. But that wouldn't happen to a town like this. It's too much of a tourist town. You can barely drive a car over the bridge to get here once the temperature goes over fifty."

"I know. But for the people who live here all year round, we care about keeping things going. You know . . . tradition."

"Mmm, I've heard that word a lot since I've moved here. You don't hear it much in cities."

"Cities are too big, too many people to care."

"Well," Lucy said, leaning over the counter, "does that mean you're going to spend your life here?"

Caroline smiled. "I don't know about that. But I want the town to be here if I decide to come back!"

"From where?" Lucy asked.

"Well, I'm saving for college. My brother, too. We're twins, so it's a double expense. Anyway, this job sure beats waitressing. You get to sit down when the place isn't busy and it pays almost as much."

"A twin?" Lucy said.

"What?"

"You're a twin!" Lucy thought twins were fascinating. People who weren't twins usually did.

"His name's Albert. But don't ever tell him I told you that! We call him Chip. Take a look out the door—he works right over there on the pier. He's

Captain Andy's assistant. Or mate, or whatever they call it."

"Who's Captain Andy?"

"Captain Andy's Whale Watch. You know. You must've seen it."

Lucy shook her head.

"Oh, you should go if you've never been. On a whale-watching trip, I mean. Those whales are fun, especially if you run into a bunch of them. Or school. Whatever. Anyway, yesterday, Chip said one doused the whole boat with the water from his blowhole! You should go on out sometime."

"Maybe I will," Lucy said.

Henry sat with his legs dangling over the edge of the pier and watched his new friend Donald fish.

"You ever catch anything here?" Henry asked. He wondered if the fish actually swam this close to the shore with all the boats and activity there.

"Sometimes," Donald replied.

Nathan sat next to his big brother, but he sat in a crouching position, as if he were poised to run.

"Hen-ry," he said for the third time since they'd sat down, and for the third time Henry ignored him.

"Please!" Nathan hissed. It was a word neither brother used often, so Henry turned around this time.

"What? Come on, Nathan, I'm busy. Go find someone to hang around with and leave me alone."

"It's im-*por*-tant," Nathan whispered. "It can't wait. I wasn't going to tell you at all, but now I have to."

Henry sighed. "Okay. So tell me."

"Not *here*."

Henry gave him an exasperated look. "Here or nowhere," he said, and looked at Donald for approval. But Donald was concentrating on his line in the water.

Nathan pushed himself closer to his brother, balanced himself on his knees, and whispered into Henry's ear, much to the older boy's embarrassment.

". . . pulled at my *blanket* . . ." Nathan whispered, ". . . called me 'Boy.' *Twice!* . . . No one there . . ."

Henry pushed his brother back. "That's looney-tunes, Nathan," he said.

"Shhhh!" Nathan said with a finger to his lips.

"No, I mean it. You've dropped a rung off your ladder, that's what."

"That's what I thought Mom or Dad would say," Nathan told him. "But not you. I thought you'd be on my side. I thought you'd come with me at night to the screen-porch to see. I thought you'd at least listen!"

Henry frowned. He might have. But that was before he'd met Donald, who delivered bread in a big truck and fished off the pier—who knew how to grab up a live, crawling, dark-brown lobster and tape its claws and throw it into a big vat of boiling water and watch it turn red! Donald was his own age, thirteen, and could not only do a lot of things Nathan, being nine, couldn't do, but he could do a lot of things even Henry couldn't do. Or at least had never done before. Given the choice, Donald won over Nathan, hands down.

"Look, Nathan"—Henry leaned away from Donald so that Donald wouldn't think *he* was crazy, too—"I'm only saying what Mom or Dad would say because I think it's true. You imagined it all. Don't be so scared and spooky. It didn't happen, okay?"

It *did*, Nathan thought.

"*Everybody* thinks what they dream up at night is real, didn't you know that?" Henry said. "Why don'tcha go over to the school playground up Main

Street?" He pointed to his left. "There're a lot of kids your age hanging around there."

Nathan's lip quivered.

"Go on. Go on, Nathan, you'll have a much better time than hanging around here with us."

There was no choice in the matter. Nathan walked away from his brother.

Chapter Five

Cousin Joan had driven the U-Haul herself, all the way from Queens. Inside the rental trailer were some cartons belonging to the Webers, as well as parkas, sweaters, turtlenecks, scarves, earmuffs and woolly hats—winter clothing that Martha had sent along thinking that they would need it "since they were living right next to the ocean, so damp and cold all the time!" Also in the trailer was everything that Joan owned: clothing, aerobics equipment, stereo, television set, records and tapes, books, linens, and whatever else she could jam into the U-Haul.

Apparently she'd cried the entire time up from Queens, because her eyes were red and black mascara streaks ran down the sides of her cheeks.

Joan arrived at four o'clock in the afternoon, at the same time the fellow organizing the family reunion came to check on the inn's facilities, and at the same time Honey the waitress decided to quit—right before the dinner hour.

Joan stood in the small lobby, arms wrapped around a box containing her stereo speakers, her blond hair, matted and stringy, slipping out of its ponytail and her large-framed glasses askew on her face.

"Hello?" she said tentatively, peering around the box she was holding. "Sandy?"

But Red was busy with the family-reunion man

and Sandy was placating Honey. They hadn't even noticed Joan. Most people didn't notice Joan.

"Honey, look. Can't you stay at least for the dinner meal?" Sandy was saying. "We can't possibly get someone before—"

"I'm sorry, Mrs. Weber," Honey answered, shaking her head, her eyelashes flapping up and down. "I'd like to help you out, but my boyfriend says we have to leave now. He had this dream, see, that if we played this one slot machine at this one hotel in Atlantic City before midnight tonight, we'd win the jackpot. I mean, it's an opportunity you can't refuse, right?"

"Honey, it's a *dream!*" Sandy wailed. "And what's more, it's *his* dream, not yours, so why can't *he* go and win the jackpot and you stay here?"

"Uh-uh, I asked him that, and he said in the dream I was with him. So I gotta go. Sorry." She was already heading for the door, but Sandy grabbed her arm and took her to a quiet corner to discuss the situation more fully.

Meanwhile, Red was having other problems.

"Mr. Weber, this place isn't as I remembered it at all," the man was saying.

"Look, Mr. Rackmill, it's been a long time since you and your family stayed here as children. The basic house is still the same, but—"

"But there's a rec room downstairs! And neat gardens where there used to be just wild grass and weeds and flowers. There's a modern *basketball court* out there, Mr. Weber!"

"I know, Mr. Rackmill—the Scottwoods put that up."

"The Scottwoods! I *knew* the Scottwoods! They wouldn't be thinking of *basketball* in their lovely old—"

"Mr. Rackmill, you knew their *parents*," Red

said, by now exasperated. "Besides, Mr. Rackmill, nothing stays the same, you know that."

"I wanted this *inn* to stay the same!"

"Hello? Red?" Joan put the box with the speakers down on a chair. "Hello, there. It's . . . me." She sniffed as her eyes filled again.

Red looked up. "Huh?" he said.

"It's Cousin Joan," she repeated. "Remember? I sent a telegram I'd be arriving today? Or maybe Aunt Martha sent it. . . ."

"Joan!" Red said. "Uh—"

"I'm sorry, Mr. Weber. This is not the Scottwood Inn my family will remember or expect to see."

"Gee, uh, Mr. Rackmill . . . did you happen to check out the rooms upstairs? I'll bet they look just the same—uh, well, pretty much. Why don't you have a look? Okay? Feel free to wander around."

"Well . . ."

"Here." Red reached for some keys from the pegboard on the wall behind the desk. "These rooms are unoccupied right now. Why don't you just go have a look?" He held the keys out to Mr. Rackmill eagerly.

"All right."

"Good. Go on, go ahead—have a good long look." Red turned to Joan. "Hi, Joan," he said in a weak voice.

"My stuff is outside," Joan said.

"Uh—"

"*Honey!*" Sandy was calling. "If you leave after dinner you can still make Atlantic City by midnight."

But it was useless. Honey was dashing out the door just as Lucy was coming in, and Honey nearly knocked her down in her haste.

" 'Bye, Luce!" she called. "Next time I see you I'll be rich!" and she was gone.

Lucy stared after her. "Where's Honey going?" she asked.

"To win the jackpot in Atlantic City." Sandy was almost in tears.

"Hi, Sandy."

Sandy turned to see Cousin Joan, her head tilted to one side, waving the fingers of one hand at her.

"Joan?"

"Uh-huh. My stuff's outside in a U-Haul. Your stuff, too. . . ."

Wearily, Sandy went to hug her cousin. "Hi," she said. "Glad to see you, but sorry it's under the circumstances . . . you know . . ."

Joan burst into tears.

"God," Sandy breathed.

"Lucy, you have to help us out here," her father implored.

"Daddy, I can't. I don't know anything about waiting tables. I'd be scared stiff."

"You think Joan would do it? She oughta be in shape from all that aerobic exercising." Red glanced over at Cousin Joan, who had propped herself against a wall and was swiping at a string of damp hair which had fallen across her eyes.

"Do *you*?" Lucy asked.

"Why couldn't this have happened earlier in the day?" Sandy said, groaning. "It's so close to dinner. Red, what'll we do?"

"Go back to New York?" Lucy asked, and batted her eyes. Her parents ignored the question but not the thought.

Red touched Sandy's shoulder and pulled her close. "Remember?" he said. "Remember when we found this place? We were thinking about Cape Cod, but everything was full. Then someone recommended going north to Cape Ann—"

"And we only had a weekend but we absolutely had to get out of the city—"

"Had to. So we packed all the kids—"

"You were in such a hurry I forgot my bathing suit," Lucy interjected, "and it turned out to be the hottest weekend in history!"

"It was your friend, what's-her-name, the travel agent, who recommended that we try the Scottwood Inn, wasn't it?" Red asked his wife.

"Mmmm. Mary. Her kids used to live near here."

"Right. And then we saw it. Even though it was August, the place reminded me of a Christmas card, with bright lights in all the windows and evergreen wreaths on the doors—welcoming all the travelers home."

"Exactly." Sandy sighed. "Welcoming people."

"And I had no bathing suit," Lucy grumbled.

"I remember that day like yesterday," Sandy said, smiling.

Red and Sandy sat on the white wicker love seat on the porch sipping Eleanor Scottwood's lemonade, wondering how to make the weekend last, how to stretch it, how to stay right on at this inn through all the seasons, watching the changes in the ocean and the sky.

"I don't want to leave here," Sandy whispered dreamily.

"I was thinking the same thing," Red said. "I can't remember when I've felt more at home. It's like this place—"

"—knows us," Sandy finished. "I've been sitting here, making believe it's ours."

"Well, it can be," Mercer Scottwood chuckled. He looked up at the sky-blue-painted ceiling above them on the porch.

Sandy and Red laughed.

"I mean it, now. If you're serious, you can sit right here through the seasons if you've a mind," Mercer repeated, and leaned back in his chair, making a steeple out of his fingertips.

He explained that he was finally ready to give the place up to the right people. He was tired. His children had escaped the Cape as soon as they could. "Eleanor, she's of a mind to see what Lake Tahoe's all about," he said, and Red rolled his eyes at his wife.

But that night, Red and Sandy had begun to talk about it. They stayed up all night talking about it, and when morning came they weren't even sleepy.

"Lucy! Henry, Nathan! We're going to buy this inn!" They woke up the children with the news.

When they told the Scottwoods, the owners showed them everything. Each room was different. One had a faded old red Persian rug on the floor and dark oak furniture; another was lighter with chintz curtains and chintz-upholstered wing chairs; one room had a big four-poster with a gauzy canopy over it and lace curtains floating on the ocean's breeze.

"Not one room has a television, did you notice?" Sandy asked excitedly.

"Yeah, you bet I noticed," Henry grumbled.

"Well, it's an old house. Old, Henry, historically old."

"I loved the climbing-rose wallpaper in Room Ten," Sandy said. "It was so old-fashioned, you could almost see a woman in hoopskirts watching it being put up."

"Mmmm," Red said, "your mother would love it."

Sandy laughed.

"Don't laugh. Can't you see Martha's reaction? If we do buy this place?"

"Red, feel the wood on this banister. Hands
have smoothed this banister for two hundred years!"

"Wait a minute," Lucy said. "Wait a minute,
guys! You are kidding, aren't you? Aren't you?"

"Well, we weren't kidding," Sandy said, ruffling
Lucy's hair. "This was what we both knew we wanted
as soon as we saw it."

"Right," Red said. "And this is what we got: no
waitress and it's dinnertime."

"I just might be able to do something about
that," Lucy said. "Caroline Wright! She's a new friend
of mine—sort of. She works at the Beach Boutique.
She told me she's been a waitress. Maybe she won't
mind helping out just for tonight."

Red looked at his daughter gratefully. "But do
you think she'd want to do this kind of work after a
long day in the shop?"

"I'll ask, but she needs the money. She's saving
for college, so I bet she'd do it. I'll run back down
there and find out what time she gets off work."

"Great, Luce, thanks. That'll solve one problem.
At least temporarily." Red went to help Joan unload
her U-Haul trailer.

Suddenly a red-faced Mr. Rackmill came blus-
tering down the stairs.

"Really, Mrs. Weber," he huffed. *"Really!"*

Sandy looked up quizzically. "Mr. Rackmill?"

"I don't think that was very funny," Mr. Rackmill
said. "Not funny at all!"

"What wasn't funny, Mr. Rackmill?" Sandy, by
this time, had about reached the end of her rope.

"My sister and I used to spend some wonderful
nights in that old screen-porch upstairs. The one
overlooking the back lawn and the ocean—"

"I know," Sandy said, and didn't remind him

that there was only one screen-porch at the inn. "My sons like to sleep there too on warm evenings."

"Well, that modern lighting you put in is just *awful!*"

"Modern lighting?"

"Those whirling lights! They look terrible in the daytime. I can just imagine what they're like at night!"

"Whirling lights?" Sandy repeated, frowning.

"And something's gone wrong with the ventilation system. It's absolutely freezing in that little room!"

"Huh?"

"Warm in the hall right next to it, but that room is just un*bearably* cold!"

Sandy's mouth hung open. She couldn't think of a thing to say.

"I'm sorry we can't come back to the place where we were so happy as children," Mr. Rackmill said. "And Mrs. Weber, if you care anything at all about running a proper inn, you'll get rid of those terrible whirling lights! Hmph! Place looks like a disco!" He stormed out.

Sandy stared after him, shaking her head. "Whirling lights," she murmured to herself. "That man's a fruitcake!"

Caroline was delighted with the chance to earn extra money. She told Lucy she got off at five and would hurry over.

"You sure you don't mind being on your feet another few hours?" Lucy asked.

"Well, I couldn't do it every night," Caroline admitted. "But once in a while won't be a problem. Anyway, you'll be there, and I'll teach you how to do it."

"Mmmm . . ." Lucy wrinkled her nose. "I don't

know. I may not even be here past the summer. It wouldn't be worth learning if I were just leaving everybody . . . you know . . ." Her voice trailed off.

"Well, I hope you stay," Caroline said. "You don't see that many new faces at school. And yours is a nice friendly one."

"Thanks." Lucy smiled at her.

"But I guess it's hard for our little town to compete with a city like New York. I guess you have a fantastic life there, huh?"

"Fantastic? Well . . . no, it's really like everyone else's life," Lucy said. "I go to school, hang out with my friends. . . . Although you can get to see the latest movies faster, that's true." She thought a minute. "I miss my grandma," she said. "A lot. But it's not as if I left anybody fabulous or anything. I don't have a steady boyfriend . . . have about three or four good girlfriends. They're all away for the summer. One's on a bike trip, two are at college summer programs for high school kids, and one's a camp counselor in Pennsylvania. But they'll all be back in the fall for school."

"And maybe you, too."

"And maybe me, too. Are you ready to go? It's five." Lucy pointed to the big wall clock. "You said you were off at five."

"Uh-huh! And lucky you, you get to meet my brother. We usually ride home after work together. Here he is. Hi, Chipper!"

Lucy glanced over at first, then stared. The boy was tall—he looked nineteen, not sixteen—his shoulders were the broadest Lucy had ever seen and he had a gorgeous dark tan. His hair was curly brown, like his twin's, and his eyes were green. Lucy looked from one to the other. Yes, Caroline's eyes were green, too, but she hadn't noticed them on Caroline.

"Hi!" Caroline went to hug her brother. "I won't

be going home with you tonight. I'm waiting tables up at the Scottwood."

"Yeah? How come?"

Caroline nodded at Lucy. "They've lost a waitress right before dinner. I said I'd help out."

"Oh. Okay. See you later." Chip headed for the door, but Caroline stopped him by tugging at his shirtsleeve. "Chipper, don't be rude. Come meet the new owner of the Scottwood. Lucy Weber. Lucy, this is my brother Chip."

"Hi," Lucy whispered.

Chip said, "The *owner*?"

"The owner's *daughter*, okay? Sorry . . ." Caroline rolled her eyes.

"Yeah, well, these days you never know," Chip said, and grinned. "Hi," he said, nodding at Lucy. "So, how do you like it here?"

"I like it," Lucy answered, and noticed she was still whispering. She cleared her throat.

"Good." Chip turned to his sister. "Saw four humpbacks this afternoon," he told her. "And they were singing. It was fantastic. The folks on the boat about died!"

"Oh—four!" Caroline said. "He means whales," she explained to Lucy. "Humpback whales. And they really do sing. But you can't always count on seeing or hearing them."

"They were playing. It was really nice," Chip said, smiling at the memory. "Well, see you at home. So long . . . uh . . ."

"Lucy," Lucy reminded him. "So long. Nice meeting you."

"Nice meeting you. Come out on the boat sometime if you haven't been." He waved and was gone.

"Maybe I will," Lucy said.

Chapter Six

Lucy sat at her desk holding a postcard from her friend Ruthie, who wrote that with all the biking her legs had developed muscles the size of a heavyweight champion's, that the scenery was nice, and that the kids on the trip were so-so.

She put the postcard down and stared out her window at the ocean. Captain Andy's Whale Watch had lasted about three hours and she had spotted one sperm whale. She had brought her camera along but had ended up taking pictures of the crew: one of Captain Andy and six of Chip Wright. Chip had been wearing cutoff jeans and a faded blue T-shirt that said SAVE THE WHALES AND DOLPHINS on the front. Maybe it was those broad shoulders that made him look older than sixteen, older than Caroline, his twin.

For his part, Chip hardly noticed Lucy. He said hi when she came on board, told her where to stand for the best views, and then left her alone. When the first and only whale appeared, Chip pointed it out to the passengers, explaining that it was "a large toothed whale with a closed cavity containing sperm oil in its big square head" and that because of the oil, this species was more in danger than other whales which were not used for oil. Lucy nodded and took his picture.

When the trip was over and they were back at

the pier, he helped her off the boat and onto the dock by holding her arm.

"Too bad we didn't get to see more," he said. "Have to try again some other time—you never know from day to day." Then she was on shore and he was buried somewhere inside the boat.

He's just some *guy*, Lucy told herself on her way back to the inn. It's the *whales* that are interesting. *He* doesn't even have any kind of *personality*! I mean, in three hours some of the boys at school would have told you their complete life histories or maybe some funny stories. Chip wasn't even friendly. So why, she wondered, did I take so many pictures of this *guy*?

Lucy left her room and started down the stairs toward the lobby. As soon as her mother, who was standing behind the registration desk, saw her, she called, "Guess what?"

"Mr. Rackmill changed his mind about the reunion," Lucy guessed.

"Mr. Rackmill? Well, no, he didn't, but it's not that. Besides, he was kind of a nut. We'll fill the rooms anyway, I hope. Did I tell you what Rackmill said about the whirling lights on the screen-porch?"

"What whirling lights on the screen-porch?" Nathan asked as he appeared in front of the desk.

"Nathan Weber, you startled me!" his mother said. "Where were you hiding?"

"I wasn't hiding, I was sitting right over there behind the vase with the cattails. What did the man say about the porch? Please, Mom, what did he say?"

Sandy and Lucy both stared at Nathan. Lucy noticed that his entire body seemed to be leaning toward them in anticipation.

"Just that we should take down the modern lighting on the porch, that it looked like a disco . . .

and that there was something wrong with our ventilation. Now, why do you want to know?"

Nathan's shoulders slumped. "Modern lighting?"
he asked.

"That's just what I said, and he told me something about whirling lights."

Nathan looked away from them and stared into
space. Whirling lights. *I* didn't see any whirling lights,
he thought. But that man did notice weird stuff on
the screen-porch. . . .

"Is the man coming back?" Nathan asked.

"No, Nathan, the man is definitely not coming
back. The inn wasn't quite the way he remembered
it. Frankly"—Sandy leaned over and tousled her son's
hair—"I think he was a little crazy, Nathan."

Nathan looked up at her. Crazy. That's what
they'd think of him if he told anyone *his* story of the
screen-porch. He swallowed, licked his lips, and wandered away.

"What's wrong with that boy lately?" Sandy wondered out loud.

"Mom," Lucy said, "you never told me your news."

"What news?"

Lucy rolled her eyes. "Mom! When I came downstairs, you said 'Guess what?' and I said—"

"Oh! I wanted you to know that Cousin Joan
came down to breakfast and was actually smiling!"

"Really?"

"Yes! And your father told a story that even
made her laugh out loud!"

"No!"

"Yes! So I've decided to go right up to her room
and tell her about my idea!"

"The aerobics classes?"

"Right! So be a sweetie and watch the desk
while I'm gone?"

"Jeez, Mom, I had something I wanted to do—"

"Oh, and we're expecting a new waitress. Her name's Clover and I'm not going to bother to interview her. If she can find the tables and she can walk, she's hired. Tell her welcome aboard."

"Mom—"

But Sandy was halfway up the stairs.

Rats! Lucy thought. I wanted to go talk to Caroline. Clover! What a name. First Honey, now Clover. She wondered if Honey *had* struck it rich in Atlantic City.

She propped her elbow up on the old pine desk and rested her chin in her palm. It was her mother's gesture.

Suddenly, Nathan's head appeared below the desk.

"Nathan, why are you creeping around this place like Herman Munster? What's wrong with you, anyway?"

Nathan took a deep breath. "Nothing," he said.

"Oh, come on, Nathan."

Nathan blinked. Twice. "Nothing," he said again.

Lucy leaned way over the desk, nearly touching her brother's nose with her own. "You know what they say, Nathan?" she said. "If you keep something bad inside, it grows into a *monster*, and if you still don't let it out, it gives you a re-al bad stomachache!" She pulled back quickly and Nathan jumped. "So, Nathan, what is it?" she asked.

Nathan frowned and looked at his shoes. He shuffled from one foot to the other. He hated stomachaches!

"Lucy, did you meet that man who saw whirling lights on the screen-porch?" he asked finally.

Lucy shook her head. "No," she said. "But he sure sounded bonkers."

"Bonkers," Nathan said. "See ya."

Nathan kicked open the screen door and shuffled out, his hands deep in his pockets. He was feeling angry. And scared. He just didn't know what to do. No one was ever going to believe a ghost pushed him out of the screen-porch by yanking on his sleeping bag and calling him "Boy."

"HELLO THERE, HOWARD!" Mr. Ainsley was rocking happily back and forth, smoothing back wisps of white hair against the ocean breeze.

"Hello, Mr. Ainsley," Nathan answered listlessly.

"COME OVER HERE! LET'S HAVE A LOOK AT YOU," Mr. Ainsley requested loudly. Nathan sauntered over. "HAH," Mr. Ainsley commented when Nathan stood directly in front of him.

"What's Howard's last name, Mr. Ainsley?" Nathan asked. He knew that Howard Scottwood was one of the Scottwoods' grown children, but he was trying to determine just how many branches Old Mr. Ainsley still had in his tree.

"Why, Scottwood, of course," Mr. Ainsley answered. He didn't yell, either. He just looked Nathan straight in the eye.

Nathan cocked his head. He twisted his lips. He tapped his foot. And then he spoke.

"Howard Scottwood is a lot older than I am, Mr. Ainsley," he said.

"That so?"

"It's so. My name is Nathan. Nathan Weber. The Scottwoods sold the inn to my mom and dad."

"Ayuh," Mr. Ainsley remarked.

"Mr. Ainsley?"

"Ayuh?"

"How long have you been here? At the Scottwood Inn, I mean."

Mr. Ainsley frowned, scratched his head, twisted his lips, looked at his lap, rocked. Nathan waited.

"Guess about . . . mmm . . .thirty years?"

"Thirty years?"

"Thirty-five, mebbe."

Nathan leaned against the porch railing. "So," he said, "when you first came here, Howard Scottwood was just a kid then, right?"

Mr. Ainsley closed his eyes and leaned back in the rocking chair. Nathan thought he might have gone to sleep.

"Howard Scottwood was about my age, huh, Mr. Ainsley?" he prodded. "Maybe younger? Mr. Ainsley?"

"Wasn't a very nice boy," Mr. Ainsley muttered. "I tried to be nice to him. Didn't help much."

"Yeah?" Nathan said. "Go on. . . ."

"Susan wasn't much nicer," Mr. Ainsley said. His eyes were still closed. "Talked mean. Talked mean to her folks."

"*I'm* not mean, Mr. Ainsley," Nathan said.

"Scottwoods were nice folks," Mr. Ainsley said. "Kids got the meanness from the old man. He was here then. Crotchety! Yelled at everybody. Yelled at the guests. Wasn't for his son and his wife, would have lost business, I can tell you."

The "old man," Nathan thought, was the last Mercer Scottwood. "Howard's grandfather?" he asked. He wanted the old man to open his eyes. "You mean Howard and Susan's grandfather?"

"Ayuh."

"Why was he so mean?" Nathan asked.

But the old man had tilted his chair back and closed his eyes. Nathan resisted the temptation to tug at his sleeve.

"Mr. Ainsley?" he said.

A long breath escaped from between the old man's lips. Nathan sighed and stepped down off the porch.

"DON'T THROW STONES AT THE GULLS, HOWARD!" Mr. Ainsley called, but when Nathan turned back, Mr. Ainsley seemed to be snoring again.

*   *   *

Lucy stood at the front desk. During the first ten minutes on duty she checked in a couple from Connecticut and their two-year-old son. They were staying overnight on their way to New Hampshire. Mrs. Rostov came a while later. She was an elderly lady in Reeboks. She announced that she spent three weeks every summer at the Scottwood. Lucy hit the front desk bell and her father appeared to take the luggage to everyone's rooms.

"Nice lady, Mrs. Rostov," Red said when he returned. "She wasn't surprised to see the Scottwoods sold the place. She knew they no longer had family who wanted it to pass it on to. Well, that's okay for us, though. We'll make it even better. Clover get here yet?"

"Clover!" Lucy giggled. "Sounds like someone's pet pig."

"I don't care what her name is, as long as she can carry a tray. Where's your mom?"

"Up there"—Lucy gestured toward the stairs—"talking to Cousin Joan about aerobics classes on the lawn."

Red chuckled and shook his head. "That idea really turned her on. I wonder how many people will want to do it."

"Daddy." Lucy came out from behind the desk. "Do you think you could watch the desk for a while? Just till Mom comes down?"

"Okay." Red nodded. "Got something up?"

"Well . . ." Lucy felt her neck flush. "I just need a break. I thought I might go down to the pier, maybe even take a whale-watch tour. . . ."

"Didn't you just do that a day or so ago?"

"Yes, but I only saw one. They say you have to—" She stopped as the screen door opened and slammed shut again. A timid-looking young girl stood framed in the entrance. She peered at them from under long brown bangs.

"Hi!" Red called. "May we help you?"

The girl licked her lips and looked down. "Mclvr," she mumbled.

"Pardon?" Red said.

The girl coughed into her hand. "I'm, uh, Clover," she said. "They said you needed a—"

"Oh, *Clover!*" Lucy cried, looking the girl over more carefully. "Our waitress!"

" 'T's right," the girl whispered. She kept her head down, her shoulders hunched.

"Oh, boy," Red said softly to Lucy. "Doesn't speak above a whisper, doesn't look at anybody . . . How's this gonna fly?"

Lucy shrugged.

"Sorry, Luce, but you'd better stay here till your mom comes down. I'll show Clover, here, the kitchen." He beckoned to the girl, but she didn't see him. Her chin was nearly resting on her chest.

"Clover?"

"Yessir?"

"Why don't you just come on back here with me, Clover. I'll show you just where everything is and what your duties will be . . . Clover? Don't be shy now. We're all family here."

Clover trudged after him, and no sooner had they gone through the door leading to the kitchen than Sandy came down the stairs with Cousin Joan. They were both babbling with excitement. Wow, Lucy thought, Cousin Joan looks almost pretty when she's excited.

"Do you have an outside outlet?" Joan was asking. "I could plug in my music—and we could mount speakers on the outside walls—"

"—take the course myself, too!" Sandy was saying

at the same time. "I always wanted to take aerobics, but there was never enough time! Lots of working women have the same problem, I'll bet. They'll *love* this!"

"—feel so much better about earning my keep now—"

"Mom," Lucy interrupted, "Clover's here. She's in the kitchen with Dad."

"Oh, good! Joan, will you excuse me for a minute? I'd better go meet her." She dashed off.

Joan stood near the desk, managed a small smile at Lucy, and shifted her weight from one foot to another.

"Hi," Joan said finally. "Guess we haven't spent much time together, have we?"

Lucy shook her head. "Hope it works out," she said. "The aerobics, I mean."

"Oh . . . yes. I hope I have more people here than I had in my class in Queens."

"Why? How many did you have?"

"Well, there was Mrs. Eschiverria . . . and Mrs. Monte . . . and Allison Reidenbougher, she was the checkout girl at my supermarket . . ."

"Yeah?"

Joan sighed. "That's all, really. And a lot of the time Mrs. Eschiverria couldn't make it."

"Oh."

They stood silently, facing each other. Lucy cleared her throat.

Finally Joan spoke again. "Aunt Martha tells me you're going back home when school starts."

"Oh. Well, I probably am. I did promise I'd give this place a chance, though. You know, so Mom and Dad can't throw it in my face that I didn't try or anything."

"Mmm, you have to try," Joan said.

Lucy peered at her. She barely remembered

Harry, but she couldn't picture Joan married to anyone.

"I guess you're feeling better, huh?" she offered.

Joan looked up. Her eyes were filled with tears. "Uh-huh," she said.

Oh boy, Lucy thought.

Chapter Seven

Henry sat down hard on one of the thick wooden pier supports and took one of the rods his friend Donald was holding out to him.

"Betcha get something with this, Henry," Donald said, "betcha get a nice snapper or something. Good eating, you'll see! You can have the cook over there at the inn fix it up for your family for dinner and they'll thank you, all right!"

Henry cast out his line the way Donald had shown him. "You really like fishing, don't you, Donald?" he asked.

"Oh, yeah. Yeah, I do. I'm going out with my uncle in August and September. He promised to take me. We're going for blues."

"Blues?"

"Bluefish. Real popular. The restaurants'll take all you can bring 'em. They—"

"Bluefish," Henry interrupted. "Blue-green with a black blotch on each side, right?"

"Yeah, that's them."

"They can run up to about four feet. They can weigh nearly thirty pounds!"

Donald frowned. "You been bluefishing?" he asked.

Henry shook his head. "Uh-uh. Just read about it. Can you catch a fish that heavy?"

"Oh, sure! So can you, Henry, you'd love it!

Your arms get strong, your face turns brown from the wind, you smell that sea air . . . It's a great life, Henry. You wanna come with us?"

"Oh, sure!" Henry grinned widely. "That'd be a great way to spend weekends!"

"Not just weekends," Donald said. "Every day. There's good money to be made in the fall."

Henry reeled in his line and looked at his friend. "How can you go every day? What about school?"

Donald shrugged. "I'm quitting, I decided. For what I'm going to do, I don't need school. I can learn everything I need to know from my uncle."

Henry looked at Donald in amazement. Quitting school! And at thirteen! "What about your mom and dad?" he asked. "Did you tell them you want to quit?"

"Yeah. They need the extra money. You don't make a lot driving a bread truck, you know? And I can bring in plenty. If my dad could stand to be on a boat, he'd be fishing with my uncle's outfit too, but he's no seaman." He looked Henry up and down. "You come out with us, Henry—in a year, you'll be looking like Schwarzenegger!"

"Come on . . ."

"You ever see my uncle? And my cousin Dan? You can learn a lot from the sea, and it's a healthy way to make a living, too."

Henry was still so stunned, he forgot to cast his line back into the water. Quit school! Work on a fishing boat instead of shuffling down the hall from locker to math class . . . Quit school, what a wild idea! He was about to discuss it further when he saw his sister coming his way down the pier. He turned toward the water, keeping his back to her, hoping she wouldn't see him. He didn't like to be noticed by his family when he was with Donald. It made him feel like a baby.

Lucy spotted Henry right away and was glad of the opportunity to dawdle there, talking to her brother, just in case anyone happened by. . . .

"Hi, Henry!"

Henry winced. Men who quit school to earn their living on the high seas didn't have to deal with older sisters who wore too much lipstick and had pink plastic clips holding up long wisps of hair behind each ear. He muttered hi without taking his eyes off the water.

Lucy sauntered over. "Catch anything?"

"Not yet," he muttered.

"Who's your friend?" Lucy asked, although she knew. Donald was the subject of many a dinner conversation.

Henry acknowledged the question with a quick jerk of his right elbow. " 'T's Donald," he said.

"Hi, Donald," Lucy said enthusiastically. And she added, to Henry's considerable embarrassment, "We've heard so much about you!" She glanced around out of the corner of her eye, but saw no one resembling Chip Wright. She turned back to Donald. "I'm Henry's sister, Lucy." She made a face at Henry. "You'd think he'd be polite and introduce us himself."

Henry offered a silent prayer that Lucy would disappear.

"Hi," Donald said, and then, "Hey!" as he reeled in his line.

"Wow!" Lucy cried.

"Flounder," Donald said by way of explanation, as he reached over to take the hook out of the fish's mouth. "Good eating." He dropped the fish into the pail next to him.

"Eee-yew," Lucy said, wrinkling her nose. "How can you do that?"

"Do what?" Donald asked, rebaiting his hook.

But Lucy just said, "Eee-yew" again and Donald knew she was queasy about the way he touched the fish and removed the hook from its mouth. He smiled to himself and hoped he'd catch another fish soon so he could impress her again.

Lucy squatted down next to the boys. Captain Andy, she figured, was due to go out again at one-thirty. It was one o'clock now. If Chip had gone somewhere for lunch, he'd probably be coming back to the pier pretty soon to help ready the boat.

"Do you eat all the fish you catch?" Lucy asked, and blinked her long lashes.

"Oh, yeah," Donald answered, "or I sell 'em. Or I give 'em away. We have neighbors who like 'em. You want this?" He reached over and held up his flounder in Lucy's face.

"Uh—thanks, but—" Lucy swallowed hard, "no thanks," she managed.

"Yeah, you probably need more than one," Donald said. "I'll send some home with Henry."

"I can catch my own," Henry said defensively. But Lucy had seen a familiar head of curly brown hair. Something turned over inside her.

"Well," she said, standing again, "be good, Henry. Nice to meet you, Donald."

She's leaving, Henry thought with relief. He dreaded hearing what Donald would say about her when she left: *Yew, how do you touch a fish. Looks like she does a lot of work with her hands.* Henry gritted his teeth. Donald was looking at Lucy as she made her way down the pier.

"She's pretty," he said. "Your sister."

Henry squinted his eyes at his friend. *"Huh?"* he said.

"Hi!" Lucy called.

Chip turned around. He had just taken a bite of

a sandwich he was carrying and his mouth was full. He nodded at her.

"Getting ready to go out again?" she asked.

"Mmm." He swallowed. "Lucy, right?"

"Uh-huh. I was thinking I'd go out with you. I mean, I only saw one whale—you know—and it was nice, but—uh—it wasn't exactly . . ." Her voice trailed. She realized she was stammering and mentally scolded herself.

But Chip Wright didn't seem to notice her discomfort. He just nodded and said, "Yeah, I know what you mean. You want to see more, see some different kinds. Whales are fun. Too bad what we're doing to them . . . to the whole environment." He shook his head and continued to walk. Lucy had to take two steps to each of his to keep up.

"Oh, I agree!" she said. "The environment. I mean, we're always talking about it at home. That oil spill in Alaska—"

Chip stopped walking. "You talk about it?"

"All the time!"

"Right," he said, "talk. But what do you *do* about it?"

Lucy's eyes widened.

"Do you protest? Do you write letters? Do you recycle? I take people out on the boat"—he waved his arm toward the ocean—"and we show them. We show them great mammals and we tell them, 'Look now, because the next generation won't be able to see them. They'll be gone, thanks to what we're doing to them. To the oceans.' I tell 'em that. They're killing dolphins and selling them for tuna—dolphins, who can be trained better than some *people*, who have intelligence higher than a lot of *people*! They're sweet-natured, too, and trusting, and we just kill 'em, so people can have what they think is a tuna sandwich!"

Lucy stared at him.

"Sorry," he said, and continued walking. "Makes me mad, is all."

"I can see that." She gulped. She had never heard him put more than one or two sentences together before this.

"You people just talk, but you don't really care enough to do anything about it. The human race'll just be living in shelters pretty soon if we don't think about what we're doing to the atmosphere." He tossed the remains of his sandwich into a litter basket. "Well . . . I gotta go," he said.

Lucy stood rooted to the spot and watched him walk away. She felt as if she had been scolded by the principal. She was actually near tears! How could he talk to me like that? she stormed inside. How could he say those things, as if I were some kind of criminal or something? She drew in her breath and stared at him as he climbed aboard his boat. Here I put on my best outfit. What a waste! I could have worn my torn cutoffs for all he'd notice.

She walked slowly back up the pier toward the main street. Well, she thought, in fairness I guess we don't really do anything about the environment. She sniffed the air. I guess it is different from New York City, if you think about it, which I didn't. I mean, the air's a lot cleaner here, that's for sure. I guess what Chip's saying is, we can't just talk about something we feel strongly about, we have to do something about it. And he is, in his way.

What do I feel strongly about? she asked herself. Chip Wright, she answered.

Chapter Eight

Nathan stood at the door of the screen-porch and swallowed hard.

It was right after supper, still early. Mom was helping the kitchen staff clear, Lucy had taken Dad off somewhere to talk, Cousin Joan was trying to unpack some more of her cartons, and Henry—well, Nathan didn't know where Henry was and he wasn't sure he cared.

Below he could hear footsteps and voices and even the clinking of dishes and silverware from the dining room. It made him feel safe. He opened the door of the porch and stepped in.

Outside it was light. Twilight was a good half hour off. He looked out over the lawn. A little girl was playing with his beach ball, tossing it to another of the guests and laughing each time the lady threw it back. Several people were walking down toward the ocean for a peaceful stroll on the beach after dinner. This wasn't a scary place, this was a nice, quiet, pretty place!

For the first time in days, Nathan began to relax. He could actually feel himself begin to unwind. He hadn't realized how tense he had felt. Coming up to the porch had taken tremendous effort, but Nathan had been determined to prove to himself that there was no ghost and even if there was, he, Nathan, was not going to let it frighten him away from the places he wanted to go. He was no coward and could stay inside the porch for at least five minutes all by himself.

And he had done it. He let out his breath slowly. Now he could go.

He turned, opened the door, and stepped outside, back into the hall. Suddenly, from inside the porch, he heard a loud *thump*. His blood froze. He whirled around, pushed open the door, and quickly glanced at every corner of the porch. It was as it had been—no one there.

Nathan closed the door again, turned his back, and listened. Nothing. No thump, no sounds at all. It was my imagination that time, all right, he thought, but he hurried down the hall to the stairs leading to the dining room.

At one end of the big lawn stood a large two-seat wooden swing, mounted on thick triangular supports. It was the one and only contribution to the inn made by Susan Scottwood, who had ordered it with her parents' permission just before she left home for college over thirty years ago. Unpainted, the wood had grown pale with age and the seat of the swing was smooth as satin.

Lucy and Red sat on it, watching twilight creep in over the ocean and idly swinging, pushing off the ground with their toes.

"It smells nice, doesn't it, Daddy?" Lucy asked softly.

"It sure does, honey, it sure does."

"And when you look at the ocean, all you can see is water and sky. No smog, no big buildings blocking the stars. . . ."

Red turned to grin at her. "You bet, Luce," he said.

"It's terrible how man is polluting his environ-

ment," Lucy said next. "Killing dolphins and baby
seals and . . . and ruining the ozone layer."

Red nodded. "Glad to see you're giving all this
some thought, Luce," he said.

They both looked up as the chunky, bustling
body of Mrs. Thatch appeared, silhouetted against
the darkening sky. She was hurrying toward them.

"Mr. Weber," she said, panting, "I have to talk
to you!"

Red stood up. "Mrs. Thatch, what is it? Now,
you come and sit right here." He patted the end of
the swing where he'd been sitting. "Tell me what's
the matter."

Mrs. Thatch sat, caught her breath, and folded
her hands in her large lap. "Mr. Weber," she said.
"Is it part of my job to stand outside in public and
move my—and move—do these twistings and turn-
ings and make these awful—"

"Mrs. Thatch—"

"—and all the time there's terrible music playing
—I mean, I never in my life!"

Lucy bit her lip to keep from laughing. "Aerobics," she said, winking at her father. "She means
Cousin Joan's aerobics class."

"Is it part of my job?" Mrs. Thatch demanded.
"To do that? Because if it is, Mr. Weber—"

"It is not"—Red held up his hand—"part of your
job, Mrs. Thatch. The aerobics classes are only for
those who wish to participate."

The large woman stood up. "Thank you," she
said.

"You're welcome."

"Because the way Mrs. Weber was talking, I got
the impression she thought I *ought* to—*had* to—"

"I'm sure Mrs. Weber didn't mean to create that
impression, Mrs. Thatch, and you do not have to
take the class."

Mrs. Thatch gave a firm nod and stalked off.

Lucy and Red both looked at each other and giggled.

"I sure am glad you're enjoying yourself here after all, Lucy," Red said, and put his arm around her shoulder.

"Huh?"

"Well . . . you're noticing the environment, how much cleaner it is here, enjoying the people a little . . ."

"Well—"

"It sure makes me feel better to hear you talking this way, honey. Because your mom and I felt awful when it looked like you were deserting us for New York and Grandma. I didn't expect it so soon, but it's great to see you adapting to the place this way. It's really just great."

"Daddy?"

"Mmmm?"

"Daddy, look, I was talking about Chip."

"Who?"

"Chip Wright. He's Caroline's twin brother. He's an environmentalist. Sort of. He's really cute."

"Huh?"

"I was thinking about something he said, that's all. About really doing something to improve the environment. I was just going to ask you what you thought about my becoming a *vegetarian*."

"Huh?"

"I mean, I'm sorry, Daddy, but I haven't made up my mind about anything yet, so please don't lay a guilt trip on me here, okay?"

She got up off the swing and headed toward the house.

The rec room in the basement of the Scottwood Family Inn was pine-paneled. It was large enough

for one Ping-Pong table and one other big table used
for extra-large jigsaw puzzles. A little room off to the
side contained a large-screen television set and some
couches and chairs so that guests could enjoy their
programs free from distraction.

On this late July evening, Red and Henry had
just finished straightening furniture, emptying
ashtrays, picking up rackets and Ping-Pong balls,
and fixing a leg on the Ping-Pong table.

"Remind me," Red said to his son, "to remind
Mrs. Thatch to remind the maid to get down to this
floor, too. Place looks like a mess every night." He
pulled out a hanky and wiped his perspiring face.
"Take a look here, son, you think this'll hold?"

"Looks okay to me." Henry shrugged.

"Yeah, you and me. Couple of city boys trying to
be handymen . . ."

"And innkeepers . . ."

"Come on, now, we'll make it. Just takes a little
determination, that's all."

"And a lot of work."

"A lot, yeah. But look, I have time for one quick
game of Ping-Pong before I have to get back up
there, so how 'bout it?"

"Naw. You always beat me."

"No, I don't."

"You do so."

"Well, it won't be long before you start beating
me. You'll see."

When I'm a little bigger, stronger, when I've
honed my reflexes, Henry thought. That can all happen a little faster if I—

He looked up at his father.

"What is it, Henry?" Red asked. "I've got to close
up the bar."

"If you had time for a game, you have time for a
talk, okay?"

Red stopped. "Okay," he said, sitting down at the big table with jigsaw puzzle pieces spread out across its top. "What's on your mind?"

Henry sat down next to him and began to fool with some of the puzzle pieces.

"Better talk, son. Mr. Grunwald will want to be getting home."

Henry fit two of the pieces together and clicked his tongue. "Okay," he said. "Dad? Do you know anything about commercial fishing?"

Red shrugged. "Not a whole lot. Why do you ask?"

"I was just thinking. Maybe it'd be a nice job."

"Well, maybe it would. I've enjoyed our little chat, Henry, but—"

"No, Dad, wait—I mean, I was thinking I'd like to be one. Maybe. A commercial fisherman."

"Well, Henry—look, you're thirteen. There's a lot of time to decide what you want to be. But what I have to be is upstairs. Okay?"

"I mean *now*, Dad. Donald's going into the business with his uncle next month. He's going to leave school and—"

"Leave school? That's against the law!"

"Well, but his folks need the money. Look, Dad, I don't mean I'd want to leave school for good. But maybe just for a year. Just to try it out. Have a real growth experience, Dad—"

"Henry, I've got to go to work up there."

"But can't we even talk about it?"

"Sure!" Red pointed his finger at his son. "Sure, we can talk. You be a commercial fisherman at thirteen years of age. You'll spend the rest of your life 'floundering' around and it'll be a 'fluke' if you ever make something out of yourself! Okay? We've talked. That's it. Now don't be ridiculous. You're thirteen. That's all." He stormed upstairs.

Henry took a deep breath and let it out. Okay I

knew he'd take it like that at first. Now I'll give it a little time to sink in and I'll start on Mom.

The screen door leading to the back porch creaked as Mrs. Rostov opened it and squinted her eyes against the bright setting sun. She tugged at her tiny flowered hat and began to make her way toward the empty rocking chair next to the one occupied by Mr. Ainsley. He didn't look up as she sat down and began to rock.

Minutes went by. Finally Mrs. Rostov leaned toward him.

" 'Evening, Edward," she said, and leaned back again.

Mr. Ainsley answered without looking up. " 'Evening, Rose," he said.

Mrs. Rostov stopped her chair and started it again so that they both would be rocking back and forth at the same time.

"Chilly tonight," Mrs. Rostov observed.

"Eh?"

"I said, it's chilly tonight!"

"I heard you, don't have to yell," he muttered.

"Stop being so cranky, Edward, this is Rose you're talking to. You can't get away with that old-geezer stuff you pull on everyone else!"

Mr. Ainsley didn't answer but he chuckled somewhere in the back of his throat.

Mrs. Rostov waited a moment before she spoke again. "What do you think of the young people who bought our inn, Edward?" she asked.

Mr. Ainsley just grunted.

Just then, Nathan opened the screen door, burst out onto the porch, and hurried across the big lawn toward the shoreline.

"DON'T THROW STONES AT THE GULLS, HOWARD!" Mr. Ainsley yelled after him.

"For pity's sake, Edward, the boy's just skimming rocks on the waves. And he's not Howard Scottwood. You know that, Edward. His name is Nathan Weber."

Mr. Ainsley grunted again.

"I *said*, the boy's *not* Howard—"

"I heard what you said, Rose!" Mr. Ainsley snapped. "Sometimes I forget."

"Howard Scottwood's all grown up now," Rose muttered, "and just as mean a businessman as he was a boy, if you ask me!"

"Didn't ask," Mr. Ainsley grumbled, and Mrs. Rostov said "Hmph" and looked away.

After a while, Mr. Ainsley said, "He looks a lot like him, though. Looks like Howard used to look as a boy."

Mrs. Rostov slapped her hands on her lap. "He looks nothing like him, Edward, absolutely nothing! It's only that he's a boy. About the same age Howard was when—"

"Forget about that, Rose, it's old business," Mr. Ainsley said.

"Hmph," Mrs. Rostov said again.

Suddenly, Mr. Ainsley began to chuckle deep inside himself. The sounds emerged like small strangled coughs. Mrs. Rostov patted him on the back.

"Don't do that, Rose!" he barked. "I was just laughing."

"Laughing? *You?*"

"I was just thinking—that boy—"

"Howard? Or Nathan?"

Mr. Ainsley waved his arm impatiently at the shore. "Him, him! That one! The new folks' boy!"

"All right, all right, you mean Nathan, what about him?"

"I have a feeling he's seen him," Mr. Ainsley whispered hoarsely, and began to chuckle again.

"Stop that. Seen whom? What are you talking about, Edward?"

"Seen *him*. You know who, Rose. Remember?"

Mrs. Rostov snorted.

"You do, you remember. Time that other young boy—the guest here, what was his name? You were here, you remember—"

"I remember no such thing."

"Sure you do. That boy sneaked out to sleep on the screen-porch one night, ran screaming out of there like a banshee! I was on my way to the john, saw that boy's face. Funniest sight, I swear, I ever saw!" He made some more of his chuckling noises and Mrs. Rostov resisted the urge to pat him again.

"It was not funny. That boy was frightened, Edward."

"Frightened of old Mercer's ghost, he was!" Mr. Ainsley laughed. "Of course, no one believed the boy. His folks just calmed him down and finished out their vacation like nothing happened."

"Nothing *did* happen," Mrs. Rostov said.

"Oh, yes it did, Rose. You know it, too. You've seen him, same as I have."

"Never!"

"Well, you won't admit it, but I will. I've seen old Mercer. Only appears to young fellers like that one there . . . and to old codgers like us."

"Speak for yourself, Edward Ainsley. You're much older than I am, anyway."

Mr. Ainsley rocked harder and smiled. "I know that, Rose, I know that," he said.

"Besides, a codger is a man," Mrs. Rostov said with a sniff.

Nathan hid the dog in his room. He prayed it wouldn't be discovered. His mom and dad never

came upstairs until late at night and Henry would
be having something to eat on the pier that evening
with his friend Donald. Henry almost never asked
Nathan to go along with him anymore.

That left Lucy, who came up to the family quarters each evening to change clothes for dinner. But
still, Nathan thought, she never bothered to come
into the boys' room for any reason. If the dog just
didn't yip or anything, it would all work out.

The dog was small. Too small, really, to be a
tough watchdog, but it was the only dog Nathan
could get and it would serve its purpose.

Red had always taught his children to read:
read to learn, for information, and read for fun.
Lucy read novels and teen magazines. The boys were
avid readers and liked to get information from books.
For his "problem" with the inn's screen-porch, Nathan had gone to the local public library and read all
he could find about the history of the inn. There
wasn't much. Mercer Scottwood built the inn in
1790. He passed it down to his son, also named
Mercer, who passed it down to *his* son, another
Mercer. The Mercer Scottwoods who were the owners when Nathan's family bought the place were the
only Scottwoods to have a son and not name him
Mercer. They named their son Howard.

So what? Nathan thought. It was about time!

He read on. The information concerned the con-
struction of the inn and what the surrounding
town and the pier had been like at the time it was
built.

Nathan skimmed. He wasn't interested in that
sort of history. But the books said nothing of hauntings. Or ghosts. Nathan asked the librarian for books
about those things but stressed he didn't want
made-up ghost stories.

"You mean books about the . . . *occult*?" the
librarian asked.

He said, "Huh?"

"*Parapsychology?*" the librarian asked. "The *supernatural?*"

"Ghosts," Nathan said.

The librarian pointed. "Over there," she said. "Aisle five."

"Thanks."

In among a small group of books, Nathan found a little volume about hauntings in houses in Massachusetts, and though it didn't mention the Scottwood Inn at all, it did inform Nathan that many times animals were the first to sense when there was a ghost in the house. They behaved differently—they whined or cried, they trembled, their ears stood straight up.

Nathan had had no trouble finding an animal. Mrs. Overton, the inn's maid, sometimes brought her old dog to work with her and kept him in one of the empty rooms while she worked. He was a sweet, placid dog and Mrs. Overton worried about his being alone all day. Nathan knew his parents ignored this small infraction of the rules because the dog was quiet and slept until Mrs. Overton was through with her shift.

So here was Nathan, in his room, petting Mrs. Overton's dog with sweaty hands while he waited for his sister to change her clothes and go down to the kitchen.

Nathan slid the dog off his lap and onto his bed. He opened the door of his room a tiny crack and peeked through. Lucy was all changed and ready for dinner, but had obviously decided more primping was necessary. She was staring into the big mirror over the fireplace in the living room, pulling at a ribbon in her hair.

Nathan checked the dog sleeping on the bed and then opened his door all the way.

"I heard them call you," he said to his sister. "For dinner."

Lucy, startled, whirled around. "You scared me, Nathan, that was a rotten thing to do." She turned and began fixing her hair again.

"But they want you down there," Nathan said. He hoped he didn't sound desperate, which he was.

"They didn't call me. They don't do that anymore, didn't you notice? You can't yell for someone in a hotel like you would at home."

"I thought I heard it," Nathan said, and looked back at the dog again.

"Nathan Weber, are you trying to get rid of me?" She said it jokingly, but was surprised at her brother's reaction.

"No! Don't be silly! No! Why would you think that? Heck, no, I don't care if you stay all night! Stay, I don't care! Do whatcha want!" He slammed the door shut and leaned against it, his eyes shut tight.

But in the other room, Lucy only shook her head. "You're weird, Nathan, you know that?" she called. "I'm going down now, and you better come, too. Mrs. Thatch doesn't like it if you're late for grace!"

He heard the door close and let out his breath. Then he scooped the little dog up in his arms and headed for the hall.

He looked both ways. The man from Room Nine and the couple from Room Eleven were dressed up and on their way downstairs to the dining room. Nathan held his breath. It must be past time for Mrs. Overton to go home, he thought. She's probably looking for her dog. . . .

"Hello, Henry," one of the men called to him.

"I'm Nathan," he replied, thinking, at least he didn't call me Howard. Clutching the dog, he headed down the hall toward the screen-porch.

Haste made him go right in without hesitating. He closed the door behind him and took a deep breath. In his arms, the dog had fallen asleep again.

"Okay, dog," he said, putting the animal down on the floor, "see what you think." He stepped back and watched.

The dog stretched. He scratched behind one ear. He looked up at Nathan.

"See anything?" Nathan whispered to the dog.

The dog blinked sleepy eyes.

All at once there was a cold draft. Nathan shivered. The dog pricked its ears. Its eyes opened wider. It seemed to be staring at something over Nathan's shoulder.

Goose pimples rose on Nathan's arms and at the back of his neck. The dog gave a little whine. Nathan began to breathe harder.

"Yap!" the dog said.

Oh, boy, Nathan thought.

"Yapyapyap!" the dog cried. It ran to the door and began to scratch at the frame.

"Okay," Nathan said hoarsely. "Okay, me too, dog." He opened the door and the dog ran out into the hall, with Nathan behind him.

"Watch out for Mr. Ainsley!" Nathan cried as the dog narrowly missed pushing the old gentleman's cane.

Down the stairs went the dog, followed by Nathan.

Mr. Ainsley leaned against the wall and watched them disappear from view. He could hear a commotion at the foot of the stairs and moved over to observe.

"Nathan! I've been looking for you."

"Sorry, Mrs. Overton."

"Really, Nathan, dinner is late, Mrs. Overton should have left ages ago."

"I'm sorry about the dog, Mrs. Weber, really."

"It's all right, Mrs. Overton, it's Nathan's fault." Sandy bent down to look Nathan in the eye. "I don't know what's gotten into you lately, young man, but I want this behavior stopped. Do you understand?"

Mr. Ainsley was watching as the little group moved away from the stairs toward the kitchen. When they had disappeared from view, he glanced over at the screen-porch. Nathan had left the door open, so he walked over to close it.

He peered into the room.

"Hello, Mercer," he whispered softly. "Up to your old tricks, I see. Well, they may not work with this boy, Mercer." The old man chuckled. "We'll see," he added. Smiling, he made his way back toward the stairs and his dinner.

Long after the dishes were done and the dining room cleaned up, Lucy sat with Caroline on the front porch. It was dark and they watched fireflies twinkling above the grass near the porch railing. Caroline was waiting for Chip to pick her up from work.

"You must be pretty tired," Lucy said.

"That's the word," Caroline said. Her leg was dangling over the edge of the porch and her head rested against one of the big support columns. "But I made over thirty dollars just in tips tonight, Lucy. That's really great. Thanks."

"No, thank *you*. You helped us out when we needed it. My parents really appreciated it, and I do, too. Anyway, it's nice to have such a good substitute waitress when each one we hire quits."

"How about tomorrow? I don't know if I can live through two days in a row, but I guess I could try."

Lucy smiled and shook her head. "No, it's okay. Bernice starts tomorrow."

"Bernice Geffner? Used to work at the laundromat?"

"I don't know. Dad found her looking for work at the ice cream place this afternoon and just grabbed her. Why?"

Caroline yawned loudly. "No reason . . . except Bernice has already had about ten jobs since school let out."

"Oh, swell." Lucy sighed.

"She's in my class, but I'm not too friendly with her."

Lucy leaned back against the opposite column. "I thought everybody would be friendly with just about everyone in a town this size," she said.

"Oh, well, you *know* everyone," Caroline said, "but I've got kind of a problem. Ever since junior high, I've been wondering who's friendly with me just because of my brother."

Lucy was glad it was dark because she knew her face had just turned scarlet.

"Chip suddenly turned into this hunk, you know?" Caroline went on. "He used to be shorter than I am, ever since we were little, and then all of a sudden—wow! I mean, you should hear the girls at school. 'His shoulders!' 'His hair!' 'His eyes!' "

"Mmmm . . ."

"We laugh about it at home, but I'm not really sure just why every girl in the school calls me up every night to get homework assignments!"

Lucy took a breath and leaned forward. "Caroline—" she began, then plunged ahead, "Chip is . . . um . . . he's gorgeous."

Caroline didn't answer. Lucy couldn't see the expression on her face.

"He is. I mean, you can't help noticing that. I noticed it."

"I noticed you noticing." Was she smiling? Lucy couldn't tell.

"But I met you first. And I liked you. First. And I still like you a lot and it has nothing to do with your brother."

"Thanks, Lucy. I really like you, too. I did right away."

"Well, I just wanted to be honest with you. I still . . . I mean, Chip's still gorgeous, though."

Caroline burst out laughing, as Chip's old blue station wagon pulled up at the curb in front of the inn. " 'Night, Lucy," she said as she stood. "Maybe I'll see you tomorrow!"

"Caroline, wait," Lucy said, following her friend down the wooden steps. "Would you want to ask Chip to come inside for some ice cream or something? Cousin Joan made it fresh this afternoon."

"I know that, Lucy. I had some in the kitchen with you, remember?"

"Yeah . . ."

"Besides, I'm really wiped. I have to get some sleep."

"Right," Lucy said, and hung back. "Sorry."

"But you can come over to the car and say hello before we go," Caroline whispered, and grinned.

Lucy blushed to her toes and hoped Caroline couldn't see it in the dark.

"Come on, Carrie, let's roll!" Chip called out the open window of his wagon.

"Hi, Chip," Lucy said, waggling fingers at him. She could see him leaning over the wheel to see her better from the passenger window. "Oh," he said, "hi. How ya doing?"

"Fine," she answered. "Okay."

Caroline got in, closed the door, and waved out the window as Chip peeled away from the curb.

He's crazy about me, Lucy thought, and trudged up the stairs and into the little hall, slamming the screen door behind her.

"Sorry," she said at the same time Sandy said, "Don't slam the door."

Chapter Nine

Sunday night, the first weekend in August. All but three of the inn's rooms were filled, even though it was the end of the weekend. But Sandy was still worried.

"We have three empty rooms," she complained to Red. "We had the place filled last weekend."

"Honey, we've never had the place filled on a Sunday night."

"We haven't?"

"No. And you're getting that city-hyper voice back. Calm down."

Sandy sighed. "Right," she said. "Tell the truth. You're not nervous?"

"No."

"I said the truth."

"Well . . . whenever we lose a waitress I'll admit to a strange feeling in my lower intestine."

"Oh, yeah, I know the feeling. And also whenever the maid doesn't—"

"And the cook doesn't—"

"And Lucy and the boys don't—"

"*And the guests don't—*" they said together, and laughed.

"Look," Red said, "it's quiet right now. Let's go outside on the lawn and enjoy that ocean air."

"What about the desk?"

"Sandy, calm down. Remember what we came

here for?" He put his arm around her shoulder.
"Lucy can take the desk. We aren't expecting anyone
tonight anyway. Come on."

Sandy groaned.

"Stop groaning. It'll all work out."

"You think?"

He squeezed her hand. "I think," he said.

Outside, they found Joan sitting on a blanket,
her arms wrapped around her knees.

"Okay if we join you?" Sandy asked, and sat
down.

"We needed a break," Red said.

Joan looked up and smiled. Red sat too, and
began to pick at blades of grass near his feet.

"That Caroline Wright is a nice girl," Joan said.
"She's a good waitress, too."

"Mm. I understand she has a twin brother Lucy
finds attractive," Sandy said. "He's an environmentalist, Red says. Works on one of the whale-watch
boats."

"That's nice."

"I'm not sure. I don't know if he knows Lucy's
alive. At least, that's the impression I get from her
mood swings. It's not easy being fifteen."

"It's not easy being thirty-something, either,"
Joan said, and then she sighed. "Mrs. Rostov was
the only one who showed up for aerobics today."

"Well, remember, we only have fifteen rooms,"
Red said. "And a lot of the guests are people who've
been coming here for years. They're here for the
ocean and The Neck and the sights, that good
seafood—you know . . ."

"Speaking of food, what we could use is a waitress who'll stay," Sandy said. "Bernice lasted three
days."

"Geraldine will stay," Red said firmly. "She guar-
anteed it." Geraldine had started work Saturday

night. She was a widow with a young son and told Red she really needed the job.

"We seem to be jinxed when it comes to waitresses," Sandy said.

"Don't even say the word 'jinx'!" Joan said. "I'm allergic to it. Anyway, let's tell Red about our new idea."

"Oh, no-ooo-oo." Red groaned and rolled over in the grass.

"Come on, Red. This is a terrific idea! And you don't have to be young to appreciate it. Mrs. Rostov and even Mr. Ainsley should love this."

"I'm not asking," Red said. "You didn't hear me ask."

"Well, I'm telling you anyway," Sandy said. "Tell him, Joan."

Joan unwound her arms from her knees and sat back on the blanket. "Okay," she said, "here it is. We've decided to start an evening book discussion group!"

Red closed his eyes again.

"Red?"

"Mmmm?"

"Did you hear? We have a nice little library in the hall on the third floor—"

"Those books are a hundred and eight years old!" Red groaned.

"I know, but they're good ones. And everybody brings along books to read when they're on vacation. We can all sit in the living room—"

"No, the rec room downstairs!" Joan said.

"Okay, the rec room, then. And say on Monday evenings, anyone who's interested can come down and—"

"People go down to the rec room for Ping-Pong," Red said. "And for TV and for jigsaw puzzles—"

"They always *did* go down there for those things,"

his wife interrupted, "and now they'll have something better to go down there for. Honestly, Red, you're being a real party pooper!"

"He's mad because he didn't think of it first," Joan said. "After all, he's the English professor."

"Hey, look, I'd love a book discussion group. I just don't know how the guests will go for it, that's all. It's good to see you enthusiastic, though, Joan."

"I just want to find something I can do that will be useful here," Joan said. "I'd like to find my . . . my place, my niche. I thought when I married Harry—"

"Forget Harry! Your place is with us now and we're glad to have you," Sandy said, and reached over to hug her.

"Say, how do you like that new mattress we got for you?" Red asked Joan. "I swapped yours for the one in Room Eleven. I mean, you've got to use it every night, but the guests come and go."

"You got me a new mattress?" Joan asked.

"Yesterday. Henry put it on your bed."

Joan shook her head.

"He didn't?"

"Well, no. The bed was just as I left it. The mattress was the same last night."

"That kid—!" Red stood up. "That tears it!" He waved his arm at Sandy. "Yesterday I also asked him to help Eddie wash the windows in the dining room and when I walked in there later, there was Eddie still all alone! I've got to have a talk with that boy!"

Henry sat on the couch, his head bent low over his lap, his hands hanging between his legs.

"I don't understand you," Red said, pacing back and forth in front of him. "This family counts on you, Henry. You're part of us. Each one of us has responsibilities. That's what it means to be a part of a family, or any group or team."

"Well, I was gonna do it," Henry said. "Only later, that's all. The thing is, yesterday was the only time we could have the whole boat to ourselves. Donald showed me around, Dad! You should see all the stuff a real fishing boat—"

"Look, Henry, Donald works for his father, too. You want to work like your friend Donald, well, you have a job, too, right here at the inn. And workers don't go off and leave their jobs when something else looks good at the moment. Now, you're grounded, Henry, for one week. You stay right here on the grounds and you work. Do you understand?"

"Da-ad!"

"Tomorrow morning, you be the first one in the kitchen when the staff arrives. I want you setting tables and busing for each meal."

"But, Dad—"

"Get your priorities straight, young man!"

Her father was busy behind the bar when Lucy came in to talk to him. She had on bright red tie-dyed shorts and a white T-shirt with SAVE THE WHALES imprinted on it.

"Looks like you're going out campaigning or something," her father noted.

"Oh, this?" Lucy looked down at her outfit. "No, not really. I mean, I *am* campaigning, but not with the outfit. I just thought the outfit looked cute." She waited. "Do you?"

"Do I what? Think you look cute?"

Lucy blushed and nodded. "Yeah," she said.

"I always think you look cute. You're my little girl," he said. Lucy made a disgusted face. "Did you

have lunch yet? Why don't you go get some sandwiches from the kitchen and bring them in here so
we can eat together?"

"Dad-dy."

"What?"

"I came in here to talk to you."

Amused, Red looked at her again. "I know," he
said. "You wanted to know how gorgeous you are
and I told you. What more is there?"

"Dad-*dee*."

Red sat up straighter. "Okay, okay. What's the
problem du jour?"

"It's serious," she said.

"I can see that."

"I think that the Scottwood Inn should under-
take something new. It will be hard at first, but it's
very important and I think we should do it."

"Okay," Red said, nodding. "What is it you think
we should do?"

Lucy clasped her hands together and began to
rock back and forth on her heels. "I think," she
said, "that we should begin a complete recycling
program of the inns trash and garbage. I've been
giving this a lot of thought, and especially in a place
as big as this we ought to do something about
making the disposal of trash as safe for the environment as we possibly can." She stuck her chin in the
air and looked her father in the eye.

"I agree with you," he said.

"You do?"

"I sure do. Your mother and I started recycling
trash when we took over here."

"Uh . . . you did?"

"You bet. The inn's been recycling since the
beginning of the summer. Haven't Henry and Nathan roped you into one of their newspaper runs
down to the center yet?"

"Well . . . they tried . . . I mean, I guess I didn't know what they were doing."

"That's what they were doing. Didn't you see the trash cans out back? One for bottles, one for food, one for plastics . . ."

Lucy shook her head. "I guess I didn't used to be—I mean, I guess I wasn't as, uh, aware of things as I am now," she said.

"Mmmm," Red said.

"So, we already recycle, huh?"

"Yup."

"Well then"—she spread her arms wide—"what *can* I do?"

"About what?"

"About the *environment*, Daddy! I mean, how can I make a difference?"

"Well, gee." Red scratched his head. "I guess you could start by writing letters to our congressmen about passing more stringent laws about cutting down on pesticides and other chemicals used in—"

But Lucy was shaking her head. "Letters are too slow, and nobody pays attention to them anyway."

"That's not true. Elected officials want to keep their jobs, you know. They need to know what people are thinking. You have to tell them what's important to you."

"Not letters, Dad. Something *else*. Something . . . you know, noticeable!"

A corner of Red's mouth turned up. "Gee, Luce," he said, "whom do you want to notice?"

"Oh . . . you know . . ." She turned and trudged toward the door. Then she looked back at him. "You sure we already recycle? Everything?"

"I'm sure."

"Oh."

" 'Bye."

* * *

Henry was stacking Number Two cans in the storeroom. He found he was sweating even though it was the coolest room at the inn. He stopped to tie a bandanna across his forehead as Lucy stomped down the two wooden steps into the room, blinking her eyes.

"How can you see anything in here?" she asked. "It's so dark!"

"Your eyes get used to it," Henry said. He went on stacking.

"So, are you mad? About your punishment?"

"Nah. I mean, I don't like it, but it was fair. I don't think it's fair that they won't listen to me, though. About leaving school."

"Oh, please." Lucy folded her arms. "They'll never let you leave school, don't be such a dweeb. And they'd be crazy to, anyway. Thirteen years old. How could you even think they'd listen to you about that?"

Henry hefted a large can onto the shelf. "Look, Lucy," he said, turning to face her. "I'm not asking to leave school forever. I'm only talking about maybe a year. I can't think of a better education than going out to sea, spending a year on a fishing boat, seeing the world—"

"Henry, your friend's uncle isn't taking his boat to Tahiti, you know. You're not going to see the world. You're going to be a very tired little kid whose muscles hurt where he didn't even know he had muscles and who's going to be way behind if and when he ever does decide to go back to school."

Henry sighed and went back to stacking.

"And I think your friend Donald is crazy and so are his parents if they let him do it. I really do, Henry. There are certain things that should come first, and school is one of them."

"Oh, yeah?" Henry looked down at her from the

top of his stepladder. "When did you start being Miss Grown-up all of a sudden?"

"It's not hard being grown up when you're around a dumb little kid brother," Lucy said with a snort.

Henry turned back to his shelves. "Get outta here," he said.

"Right," Lucy said, "fine!" and stormed out, only to reappear a moment later. "Henry?"

"*Now* what?"

"I forgot. The reason I came looking for you."

Henry pulled off his sweaty T-shirt and tossed it to the floor. "Can't wait to hear," he said.

"Can you help me with a project? Something that's good for the ecology?"

Henry started to say *Yeah, close your mouth,* but he resisted. "Like what?" he asked instead.

"I don't know—anything! Please, Henry?"

Henry pulled the last can out of the last carton and hoisted it up onto the shelf. He sat down on an empty crate, took off his bandanna, and wiped his forehead and cheeks with it.

"What's the sudden interest in ecology?" he asked.

"Shouldn't everybody be interested?"

"Well, yeah, they should. But I never figured you would be."

"Why?"

"Because you're so interested in yourself, that's why."

"Oh, and you're not!"

Henry stood up. "Yeah, maybe I am, but not like *you*," he said.

"Well, thanks a lot for all your help!" Lucy said, and began to storm out again.

"Okay, okay," Henry said. "What about dioxin?"

Lucy turned around. "What's dioxin?"

"It's a bunch of chemicals. It's dangerous because just a tiny bit of it in the system causes all
kinds of bad stuff. Birth defects, the breaking down
of the immune system, all kinds of diseases. It's real
bad. It's in pesticides, wood preservatives, it gets
into our water supply, the food we grow, it's in the
containers that hold our milk—"

"Hey, that's terrible!"

"Yeah, it's terrible. So why don't you do something about it? If you're really looking for something
to do, I mean."

"I am! But what can I do about that?"

"I don't know! You asked me about making the
environment better and a way to make it better is to
ban dioxin, so that's what I told you. Go ban it,
Lucy, and leave me alone already!"

Nathan put his egg-salad sandwich on a paper
plate, dumped two large chocolate chip cookies on
the plate with it, picked up a container of milk, and
opened the kitchen door with his foot in order to
take the whole thing outside.

He caught the door against his back so it
wouldn't slam on his arms and began the long walk
across the lawn toward the ocean.

Behind him he heard, "HOWARD!"

He kept walking. He didn't want to engage in
one of those disjointed conversations with Mr. Ainsley
again. He could never tell whether the man knew
who he was and was just teasing him or really had
no idea whom he was talking to.

"HOWARD!"

Nathan caught his lip between his teeth. It was
hard to pretend you didn't hear when someone called
you . . . although Lucy and Henry seemed to do it all
the time.

"NA-THAN!"

Well, that did it. Nathan stopped, turned around.

Mr. Ainsley and Mrs. Rostov were waving to him from the porch. They were both smiling. And now they were beckoning. At least, Mrs. Rostov was.

Resigned, Nathan trudged slowly back toward the inn and climbed up the porch steps. "Hi, Mr. Ainsley," he said. "Hi, Mrs. Rostov."

"Hello, Nathan, dear," Mrs. Rostov said. "Why don't you sit right here"—she rose from her rocker—"and have your lunch? I'm going inside and Mr. Ainsley would like a word with you."

"I would not," Mr. Ainsley grumbled.

"Yes—you—would," Mrs. Rostov prodded, emphasizing each word.

Bewildered, Nathan sat in the rocker, put his plate on the floor, picked up his sandwich, and took a big bite.

"Mr. Ainsley wants to apologize for teasing you all the time," Mrs. Rostov said. "He knows who you are."

"Not al-ways," Mr. Ainsley said firmly. "He looks just like young Howard Scottwood."

"No, he doesn't, and Howard Scottwood is not young! Now before I go back inside, I want to hear you apologize to this poor boy. You must be driving him crazy!"

Nathan chewed, swallowed, and took another bite.

"Edward," Mrs. Rostov said, "I'm not leaving this porch until I hear it."

"Oh, Rose—"

"Go on!"

"I know your name, it's Nathan Weber. I'm sorry if I bothered you," Mr. Ainsley said. He didn't look at Nathan when he said it.

"It's okay," Nathan said, his mouth full.

"'Now, go *on*, Rose, go take your nap!" Mr. Ainsley said, brushing at her with his fingers.

"I'm not taking a *nap*! I'm taking *aerobics*!" Tsk-tsking, Mrs. Rostov flounced inside.

"Uh," Nathan said, "was that it, Mr. Ainsley?"

But Mr. Ainsley was staring into space and didn't seem to hear Nathan.

"Well, 'scuse me, then." Nathan began to back off the porch.

"You've seen him, haven't you?" Mr. Ainsley asked, still staring straight ahead and not at Nathan.

Nathan dropped his milk container and didn't even notice the white puddle at his feet.

"Old Mercer's ghost, that's what we're talking about, isn't it, Nathan?"

Nathan gulped.

"It's been a while since I've gotten a good look at him. But there's no mistakin' who he is, no mistakin' him at all, no sir."

Nathan found he could hardly breathe, much less answer. He could feel his eyes getting wider and wider. He wondered if they could actually pop. Eyes in the comic books popped. . . .

"You been thinkin' you're crazy, right? *Right?* Yep, I know. Well, you're not crazy, Nathan, not crazy at all. Mercer haunts that porch and you and I know it and Rose, she knows it, too. There's some little young one was a guest here a few years back and he knows it, too, and maybe some more, for all I know."

Nathan started to speak and choked. He coughed and coughed and Mr. Ainsley struggled up from his rocker to pat him on the back. Then they both sat down together on the porch steps, taking care to avoid the spilled milk.

"I'm not crazy," Nathan said breathlessly. "You, you're a grown-up and you know, you've seen, I'm not crazy, right? I mean—"

"You're not. I said." He nodded and patted Nathan's knee.

"Well, but—" Nathan looked around, "is it really Mercer Scottwood? Really?"

"Yeah, but you got to keep them straight. This Mercer's young Howard's grandfather. The father of the feller your folks bought this place from. Not the original Mercer, the one who built it, see?"

"Yes, but why is he there? And how come I'm the only one that sees him? I mean, there was this guest who saw whirling lights, but he didn't say anything about a ghost, and Mom and Dad've been around the screen-porch lots of times, I've seen 'em, and even the maids vacuum—"

"Whoa, whoa, boy, hold it! Listen here. Seems old Mercer only shows himself to young ones and old fogies. Kids, mebbe, because he thinks it's Howard come back and he wants to scare the pants off him. Old ones, well, here's what I think—I think he just feels comfortable with old folks. He was pretty old when he passed on, y'know."

Nathan shook his head.

"Now, I never woulda said a thing to ya. People'd put an old geezer like me in a home right away, lock him up. You know how people are, think the minute you pass the retirement age you lose every bit of sense you ever had. So you can just imagine if I started talking about ghosts in the attic, can't you, boy?"

"The screen-porch."

"Just an expression, boy, just an expression. But I decided to talk to you about it because I knew, I just knew you'd seen what you'd seen. Understand?"

Nathan nodded. "It scared me, though. It scared me real bad. And Mrs. Overton's dog, too."

"Yeah, I saw that." Mr. Ainsley chuckled. "Poor

little tyke. Hear he won't let the woman bring him back to the inn now."

"Oh. That's why we haven't seen him around. . . ."

"So tell me, boy. What does old Mercer look like? Same as when he died?"

"I never saw him when he died, Mr. Ainsley," Nathan said.

Mr. Ainsley looked bewildered for a moment. "Oh, ayuh," he said, "that's right, that's right. . . ."

Nathan brushed sandwich crumbs off his knees and stood up. "So how come," he asked, "Mr. Mercer wants to scare the pants off Howard Scottwood?"

"You got a match, son?" Mr. Ainsley asked.

"A match? What for?"

"My *pipe,* son, what else?"

"Mr. Ainsley, you don't *have* a pipe," Nathan said. "And I think you just don't want to tell me!"

At that, Mr. Ainsley rocked way back in his chair and laughed out loud.

"Tell me, Mr. Ainsley," Nathan begged. "Please."

"Son, you just never mind about all that. It happened a long time ago and it's not even important now. Make a good ghost story it would, though, sometime."

"Will you tell it to me? Sometime?"

But Mr. Ainsley was lost again in his own thoughts and had begun to look out at the ocean.

"Will you come there with me?" Nathan asked, tugging at Mr. Ainsley's pants leg. "Mr. Ainsley, will you come to the porch with me? Later, maybe? Another time, maybe? Will you?"

The old man rocked back and forth. "Listen to that, Howard," he said. "Listen to the sound the waves make, crashing against them rocks like that. Listen, boy. Calm your restless mood."

Nathan gave up. For the moment.

Chapter Ten

"I think I've got something," Henry said, beginning to reel his line in. He and Donald were in their usual place on the pier, dangling their legs over the side and watching the water as well as the tourists who visited the shops and tour boats.

"Yeah? What?" Donald asked.

Henry pulled it up. "Great. It's a piece of an old life preserver. That's the second time I've pulled up junk."

"It's not going to get any better, either," a voice said above them. Henry looked up to see Chip Wright shaking his head.

"Yeah." Henry sighed. "I know. The greenhouse effect."

"Yup . . . it'll affect the phytoplankton. We lose the krill, then we lose all the creatures that depend on it: penguins, seals . . ."

". . . dolphins and whales . . ."

"What are you guys talking about?" Donald asked, frowning.

Chip turned to him. "*Krill*, Donny. You know what krill is?"

"Uh—"

Henry answered for him. "Tiny crustaceans. They're food for larger species. When the ozone layer is depleted, the excess ultraviolet light reduces their productivity."

"Get it?" Chip said. "No food. No food, no life."

"Well," Henry said, "at least they're going to do something about Boston Harbor. They're going to compost all the city's sewage sludge."

Donald made a face. "Come on. Sewage sludge . . ."

"No, this is important, Donald," Henry said. "Did you know that the total volume of sewage pouring into the bay is higher than the volume of all the tributaries put together? The Charles, the Neponset, the—"

"Gimme a break, who cares?" Donald said. "I didn't come out here for a history lecture."

"It's not a history lecture, goober!" Chip said, and whacked his fingers lightly across Donald's shoulder. "It's something that affects you. Personally. You ought to care about that. Especially if you're going to be a fisherman."

But Donald just sneered. "I know how to work a boat and I know how to use the equipment. I don't need to know any more than that. And neither does my uncle. He does okay." Donald stood up. "I'm getting a hot dog. You coming, Henry?"

"Times change, Donny," Chip said. "You're going to need to know more than your uncle did. . . ." But Donald was already stalking off down the pier.

"I don't think he likes to be called Donny," Henry said, starting to follow his friend.

"Yeah, well, my sister and I taught him how to use a potty, so he'll always be Donny to me," Chip said. "You better catch up with him. What he really doesn't like is thinking maybe he doesn't know everything there is to know."

Henry glanced once at Chip and then began to hurry toward the pier entrance. "Hey!" he called. "Wait up!" He reached Donald as they turned onto the street and grabbed at his sleeve. "What's the matter with you, anyway?" Henry asked, panting.

"Nothing."

"Yeah, right."

"Listen, you wanna get something to eat or not?" Donald asked. "Because I don't care if I eat by myself. Maybe I'd even like to eat by myself."

But Henry tagged along after him. "I don't get it," he said. "What'd I do, anyway?"

Sandy patted the seat next to her on the couch. "Sit," she told her husband.

"Can't, babe. I have to go over this week's orders for the bar. Just came down to see how the book discussion group was going."

"I know," Sandy whispered. "I should be in the kitchen, but I wanted to check things out." She looked across the room at Cousin Joan, who sat gloomily in the easy chair. "Not one person came."

Red made his voice light. "Say, Joan . . . maybe the folks didn't see the posters we hung up?"

"Or maybe they did," Joan said with a sigh. "I thought it would be interesting to discuss *All the President's Men*. I mean, even though it happened years ago, there's always corruption in government and the Nixon years could still make for lively discussions . . ." Her voice trailed.

"I thought we should have picked a classic," Sandy grumbled. "Like Dickens or Mark Twain."

"*That* would have brought them running," Red said, and his wife smacked his arm.

"Well, more importantly, we got our new and final waitress just now," Red said. "So there's the good news."

"I can't keep them straight," Joan said.

"This one is Alice Marie. I know she'll stay."

Joan and Sandy gave each other a look as Mr.

Ainsley and Mrs. Rostov came into the rec room arm in arm.

"Good evening," Mrs. Rostov said, smiling.

"Mrs. Rostov, would you care to join us for a book discussion?" Joan asked. "How about you, Mr. Ainsley?"

"Oh, thank you, dear," Mrs. Rostov said, "but we came down to see if we could get any more of Yellowstone Park."

"I beg your pardon?"

"The jigsaw!" Mrs. Rostov pointed to the big table in the center of the room. "We both figured it's got to be the geyser, Old Faithful. With lots of park in the background. We wanted to do the sky tonight." She nodded. "That's the hardest part. All blue."

"Enjoy yourselves," Red said.

"Maybe we should have picked a current novel," Sandy said. "A best-seller. *That's* what we should have done."

Red turned to leave. "Well, why don't you guys discuss *All the President's Men*? You remember that time really well!"

"Red, it's not for *us*. It's to bring together the guests of the inn! It's an extra added attraction of the place. No other inn or hotel offers anything like it. *I* know—we just didn't advertise it well enough. Next week, I'm going to put fliers in everyone's room!"

Red headed out the door. "That should do it," he muttered to himself.

Chapter Eleven

Lucy was behind the front desk talking to her grandma on the phone when a family of four came into the lobby. She knew she should hang up to help them, but she didn't want to. Martha was giving her bruised ego a much-needed boost.

"How can he help but notice you, darling? Even in a big city like this everyone noticed you. Now, weren't you one of the most popular girls at school?"

"We-ll . . ."

"Of course you were. I've seen the girls and boys flocking to your apartment—why, even over here! Remember just before you moved, everyone was stopping over here to say good-bye and bring you little presents—"

"But he hardly *notices* me, Grandma. I mean, he's polite and everything, but that's where it ends!"

"These things take time. You'll see. When school starts again and the whales go back into hibernation—"

Lucy giggled. "I have to go now, Grandma. I have to check some people in."

The young girl in the family looked about the same age as Lucy and she was red in the face as she glowered at her parents. The other child, a boy about Nathan's age, was sitting on one of their suitcases as the others argued around him.

"It's a boring place," the girl said, making a face as she glanced around.

"Boring!" her mother snapped. "You haven't even gotten to your room yet, for heaven's sake. This is a beautiful old inn, with—"

"A beautiful old inn is for old people, not kids! There's nothing to do, and I want to go home!"

Lucy's hand, poised over the register, began to tremble. She was more than relieved to see both her parents coming toward her from the dining room.

"Hi," Red said, holding out his hand. "Red Weber. You must be the Jordans."

The father shook his hand. "Matt," he said. "My wife Betty, my daughter Karen, my son Ted." He wiped the sides of his mouth with his handkerchief. Lucy could tell he was angry and embarrassed.

"Have you registered yet?" Sandy asked. "Our son Henry will take your bags up to your room."

"I can't think of one good reason to stay," Karen said. She began to tap her foot impatiently. "There isn't a thing for someone my age to do here. You might have thought of *me* when you made these plans." She gave her father a disgusted look.

Red and Sandy exchanged glances.

"Uh," Red began, "actually there are a lot of things to do. Swimming, fishing, sports, sights to see, hiking . . ."

Lucy put her pen down and came out from behind the desk.

"Look," she said, "there's a great shopping area down by the pier. I'll show it to you. And afterward, I'll show you where there's a terrific beach. You can improve on your tan."

Sandy put her hand on Lucy's shoulder and squeezed it.

Karen looked Lucy over. "Well . . ." she said.

"Go on up to your room and change into your

suit. We can bike over there. The inn has guest bikes. By the way . . . I'm Lucy."

Karen's scowl disappeared. "I guess that sounds cool," she said. "Karen."

As the Jordans made their way upstairs, Sandy smiled at Lucy, then gave her a massive hug. "That was wonderful!" she cried.

"Oh, it's okay, Mom. I really kind of felt sorry for Karen, though. Here she was, just brought here— she missed her friends and her home—"

"She was pretty rude to her parents."

"She was pretty mad."

"Yes, but see? If she just keeps an open mind, she might have a good time. Already she's met *you.* Change doesn't have to be a bad thing. Right?"

Lucy smiled at her.

"Right, Luce?"

"No, it doesn't have to be bad. 'Bye, Mom, I'm changing into my bathing suit."

"Lucy," Sandy called after her, "thanks!"

Karen's brother, Ted, came out of his room on the second floor bouncing the basketball he'd brought. His father had noticed an old hoop mounted over the doors on a storage shed at the other end of the back lawn, and Ted loved to shoot hoops more than almost anything else.

As he neared the stairs leading to the lobby, he stopped. There was a boy, about his own age, sitting on the floor, facing one of the rooms.

"Hey," Ted called. "Wanna play ball?" He bounced the ball as he walked toward him. "What's your name?"

"Nathan Weber." Nathan looked up at the tanned boy dribbling his basketball. "I don't think you should bounce that inside," he said.

Ted caught the ball. "Sorry," he said. "Are you staying here, too?"

"I live here," Nathan said, and eyed the new boy.

Seems Mercer only shows himself to young ones and old fogies . . .

"How long are you staying?" Nathan asked. "Just the weekend?"

"No," Ted said, "the whole week."

"No kidding! That's great!"

"Why?" Ted asked.

Because now there are two "young ones," Nathan thought. Aloud, he said, "What's your name?"

"Ted Jordan."

"Nathan Weber."

"Yeah, I know. You said. You want to shoot hoops?"

Nathan didn't, but if he was going to drag Ted into a haunted room, the least he could do was play Ted's game.

"Okay," he said. "Sure, we'll shoot hoops."

Lucy and Karen bought brown-rice-salad sandwiches at the health-food store and munched on them with Caroline at the Beach Boutique. Karen bought a bathing suit that made Lucy gulp at the price and used her father's credit card to pay for it.

"Thanks for bringing me a customer, Lucy," Caroline said, winking at her. "You've been a deadbeat all summer."

"I don't know anyone who can afford this stuff," Lucy said.

"My dad wants me to be happy," Karen said. "He said I could buy whatever I wanted."

They all looked up as the bell over the door tinkled and Chip came in.

"Hi, Chipper," Caroline said. "Your lunch is in the back. Help yourself."

"O-kay!" He headed for the small refrigerator in the store's small office.

"I fixed it for him today," Caroline told Lucy. "He left in a hurry this morning."

"Who's he?" Karen asked, staring after him. "A friend of yours?"

"Sometimes," Caroline said, smiling. "Actually, he's my brother."

"He's cu-te," Karen whispered to Lucy, who felt a tightening in her chest. "Where's he going?" Chip, carrying his lunch, gave them a little wave as he headed out the door.

"Just down the pier to Captain Andy's boat," Caroline explained. "He works on the whale-watch."

"Oooooh. Let's go on it, Lucy," Karen said eagerly.

"I've been," Lucy said, and began to examine some strings of beads on a rack.

"It sounds like it might be interesting," Karen said.

"It's not that great," Lucy said.

"Do they have them every day?"

"Yeah."

"Well, I'd like to do it before we go." She went to the door of the boutique and looked out toward the boat.

"Well," Caroline said, and cleared her throat, "how's Alice Marie working out?"

"She's still there so far," Lucy said. She was watching Karen watch Chip.

"Come on, she's only here for the week," Caroline said, patting Lucy's arm.

"Yeah. That's not enough time to fall in love, is it?"

Caroline smiled. "It was time enough for you, wasn't it?"

*   *   *

Henry hurried to keep up with Donald, who seemed to try to get out of his way at every opportunity.

"What're we going for today, Donald?" Henry asked. "What do you want to catch?"

"I don't care," Donald said over his shoulder. "I'm going to hang around, wait for my uncle's boat to come back . . . see if I can help. You don't have to come if you don't want to."

"Hey!" Henry stopped walking, making Donald stop too. "What's the matter with you, anyway? What did I ever do to you to get you sore? I'm having a hard enough time with my father, trying to get the year off to go fishing with you and your uncle, without you starting in on me, too. What's going on, anyhow?"

Donald blew out his breath, lifting a cowlick off his forehead. "Your dad will never let you quit school," he said. "You're too smart. You know stuff. Your dad probably wants you to go to college and everything, too, huh?" He seemed to say it with a sneer.

"Yeah," Henry said defensively, "probably. Well, yeah, he does. But I guess I want to go, too. I mean, it's not just my dad."

"Yeah, well, you see?" Donald's chin was sticking out. "I'm not like you. I'm gonna be a fisherman, and I don't need school. What I'm gonna do—maybe someday—I'll get me a nice charter-boat business and take out rich people who wanna catch marlin and sailfish and I'll live someplace warm where you can go out all the time."

"The Caribbean?" Henry asked.

"The what?"

"You don't even know the—" He stopped talking when he saw Donald's face darken. "Look, Donald," he began, but his friend just turned and stalked away from him.

"I hate school," Donald muttered. Henry had to strain to listen. "I really hate it, listening to stuff you don't even need in your life. Who cares about old kings and dates and nouns and verbs and what *X* means! I don't use any of that stuff and neither do you, Henry, so you don't need to show it off!"

"I'm not showing off!" Henry cried, too loudly, surprising them both. "Listen—you know a lot of stuff I don't know."

"Oh, sure."

"No, you do. Besides, it's fun, hanging out with you."

Donald made a disbelieving face.

"Hey, look." Henry crossed his fingers, hoping his parents would say what he was about to do was all right. "Why don't you have dinner with us? Up at the inn . . . it's fun! There are always a lot of people around, the food's good when my sister doesn't help with it . . ."

Donald just looked at him, but his features softened.

"I mean it, Donald. Anyway, I want you to talk to my father. About fishing. About working on your uncle's boat. Tell him what it would be like, the fun we'd have, the stuff we'd learn. Come on, Donald."

Donald shuffled his feet. "I can't tonight, I have to help my father make late deliveries."

"Okay, then, tomorrow. Wednesday! *Thursday!* I don't care, you pick a night."

Donald bobbed his head slowly. "Okay, I guess Thursday's okay."

"Okay, great. Now, can we fish before the boats come in?"

"I guess. There's your sister."

They both watched Lucy walk by with Karen. Lucy waved at them.

"Will she be there? At the inn for dinner Thursday?"

"Who, my *sister*? She's *always* there," Henry said. "Why?"

"I was just wonderin'."

Joan was taking desk duty when Mrs. Thatch approached. " 'Scuse me," the housekeeper began, "but do you know where I can find Mrs. Weber?"

"Oh, I thought she spoke to you, Mrs. Thatch. She went in to town to see about the new bedspreads for upstairs. Can I help you with something?"

Mrs. Thatch looked Joan over. Certainly looked better than when she come, Mrs. Thatch thought. Lost the red around her eyes, hair isn't so stringy . . . mebbe even gained a little weight. Well, but no, she still doesn't look like she could handle much of anything. . . .

"Thank you," she said, "but I guess I'll wait for Mrs. Weber."

"Oh," Joan said pleasantly, "all right."

But as soon as she'd taken two steps, Mrs. Thatch stopped. This shouldn't keep, she thought. The boy's not at all like young Howard, but you never know with these young 'uns how they'll turn out when something gets in their heads at an early age! They can go on and tell me it's none of my business, but at least I can look myself in the mirror and say I tried.

"Miss, uh . . ." she began.

"It's all right if you call me Joan, Mrs. Thatch."

"Ayuh. Well. It's about the boy. Young Nathan."

"Oh?"

"The maids. They say he follows them."

"*Follows* them?"

"Ayuh. When they clean up the screen-porch up

on the second floor. Seems like he's waiting for them. Goes inside with them, stays there while they vacuum. Well, there's not much to do there since no one hardly ever goes in, always so drafty, you know, but young Nathan, well, he just stays there. And he stares."

"Stares at what?"

"Don't know. The maids don't know. Just seems like he's looking at something. Or looking *for* something. Never says a word. Strange behavior for a young 'un, you ask me. Yesterday he brought that young guest from Twelve in there with him. Nary a word to him, either."

"Thank you for telling me, Mrs. Thatch. I'll tell his mother."

"You do that, you be sure to do that. Can't seem to have good luck with young boys in this house somehow. Now, this one started out real good, I'd hate to see him go sour."

Joan nodded. "Thank you," she repeated.

"Thought someone should know."

"I appreciate it."

"Ayuh. Well. Sorry I couldn't go to that class of yours."

"That's all right, Mrs. Thatch."

"My back. Have a bad back."

"Really, it's all right." Joan smiled at her.

Chapter Twelve

On Thursday morning, Lucy opened her eyes and looked toward the window. The sky was overcast.

Good, she thought. Karen has been wanting to go out on Captain Andy's boat but she can't do it today. It's going to pour!

Is she Chip's type? Lucy wondered. It doesn't look like I am, that's for sure. And Karen isn't anything like me, so maybe she is. Well, she's only here until Sunday—three more days, really. I guess I can live with it.

When Henry's radio alarm went off, the first thing he heard was the weather report. He threw on his shirt and jeans and hurried downstairs to talk to Red.

"Hey, Dad!"

"Hm?" Red was leaning over Sandy's shoulder as they checked registration on the inn's computer.

"Did you hear there's a hurricane watch on for today?"

Sandy looked up from the computer screen and glanced at the window. "It's not even raining, is it?"

"It will," Henry said. "I mean, that's what the radio said. A watch for the Cape."

Red stood up straight and stretched his long

arms. "Well, it is getting toward late August," he said. "And that's the time for it."

"I know, but never right on the ocean like this. It should really be interesting, shouldn't it?"

"Oh, fascinating," his mother said, rolling her eyes. "Can't wait!"

"I think I'll go get Donald and bring him up here. No one'll be fishing today, anyway. Besides, he's supposed to eat dinner with us here tonight, so he'll just stay."

"I don't remember your inviting a friend for dinner tonight," Sandy said.

"Oh—well—didn't I tell you? Sure, I did, Mom. I mean, is it okay?"

"Donald is the boy who's quitting school to be a fisherman," Red told his wife.

She said "Oh" and looked at Henry.

"He's a great kid, Mom!" Henry cried.

"You're not leaving school, Henry," his mother said, and went back to the computer.

"I'm just asking about *dinner*," Henry complained, flinging his arms in the air.

"All right, all right, have Donald stay for dinner," Sandy said, "but forget about leaving school."

"Sheeesh!" Henry said, and let out a loud sigh.

Nathan lay in bed and blinked his eyes. Cloudy, he thought. Maybe Ted wouldn't want to play basketball, for a change. Maybe he'd want to stay inside. Play Ping-Pong, do a jigsaw puzzle, watch TV . . . read comics out on the screen-porch. His mother had told him to stop following the maids in there, but if he went there alone with Ted—just to read comics, of course . . .

He sat up. Maybe Mr. Ainsley would like to sit out there with us, he thought.

* * *

Lucy and Cousin Joan were folding linen napkins in the dining room when Joan stopped and went to the big windows overlooking the ocean.

"You know, it's getting real dark out there," she noted, frowning.

"Henry says there's a hurricane watch," Lucy said.

"Yes, I know. That's why Alice Marie isn't coming in."

"Alice Marie isn't waiting tables for lunch?"

Red came in then from the kitchen carrying wooden bread trays. "No," he said, "she's afraid of driving in the storm. And Mrs. Thatch isn't coming either."

"Mrs. *Thatch*?" Lucy asked. "She never misses a day!"

"Yes." Red nodded. "She says she misses hurricane days and the anniversary of her late husband's death."

"That's sweet," Joan said with a sigh.

"What about lunch?" Lucy asked. "Will we have a buffet, or what?"

"Lucy, do you think you might wait lunch? Just this once?" her father said. "I know Caroline showed you what to do."

"Aw . . ."

"Come on, Luce."

"Okay. But did Alice Marie say anything about tonight?"

"I imagine," Red said, "that if she's afraid to drive during the day, the night isn't going to be any more appealing. Why don't you give Caroline a call at the store and see if she'd want to come up tonight, give us a hand?"

"I'm so bored!" Karen cried. She was pacing the floor in the inn's big living room.

"Karen, please," her mother said.

"But there isn't a single thing to do-oo! Nobody even wants to go downtown! I mean, what's a little *rain*storm, anyway?"

"Karen, please," her mother said.

"Daddy, come *on*. Let's go somewhere! Lucy can't even go out, she has to *work*, they're making her *work. Think* of something to do!"

"Karen, please," her mother said.

Mr. Ainsley and Mrs. Rostov sat in the big couch at the other end of the room. Mrs. Rostov was doing needlepoint. Nathan squatted on the rug at their feet.

"Mr. Ainsley?" he said.

"What is it, dear?" Mrs. Rostov answered for him.

"I want to go to the screen-porch today."

Mrs. Rostov glanced at Mr. Ainsley and went back to her needlepoint. "Whatever for, Nathan?" she asked.

"Because there's another kid here, just my age. And Mr. Ainsley's here . . . and nobody's going anywhere because of the storm . . . and I just want to. I think we should."

"Why?" Mrs. Rostov asked.

"Because I want someone else there when the ghost comes. I want other people there, so I'll know they see him, too."

Mr. Ainsley's eyes were closed and Nathan wondered if he was asleep.

"Edward never told you there was anything to fear from the screen-porch, now, did he, Nathan?"

Nathan nodded firmly. "Oh, yes, he did. And he said you saw it, too!"

Mrs. Rostov turned pale.

"What happened, Mrs. Rostov?" Nathan asked. "What was so awful that Mercer Scottwood stays there and waits for little kids to pick on?"

"Nothing," Mrs. Rostov said. "Nothing at all. Never heard anything so silly!"

"He's waiting for Howard, so he can get even with him," Mr. Ainsley said, his eyes still closed. "That's what he's doing there." He lifted his cane slightly and banged it on the floor.

"For *what*?" Nathan asked, sitting down on the rug. "What does he want to get even with his grandson for?"

"That's just stuff-and-nonsense!" Mrs. Rostov said, and sniffed.

"No, 'tisn't, Rose, no, 'tisn't. Old Mercer was mad as hell when it happened, and he's never got over it!"

"Watch your language. There's a child here!"

Mr. Ainsley's eyes were open now, and he was looking directly at Nathan. "Howard Scottwood was a mean, ornery boy," he said, narrowing his eyes at Nathan. "Just as soon throw a stone at you as look at you. And I know, 'cause I seen him do it, lots of times. What he did was, he knew the old man kept cash under the floorboards of the old screen-porch. Cash and some of his mama's jewelry, handed down to her from the first Mercer's wife. Supposed to have brought it over on the *Mayflower*, some said. Young Howard, he stole it all."

"He stole his grandfather's *money*?"

"And the jewelry. No one ever saw it again. Except for one necklace. Thing is, Howard wasn't content just to have the treasure—oh, no. He wanted his grandfather to know who done it. Wanted to taunt him with the whole caper, see what I mean? One night, Howard went back up there to the porch with this one necklace—gold it was, right, Rose, with little emeralds?"

"Rubies," Mrs. Rostov said.

"Rubies mebbe. Anyway, there was Howard up on the porch. Had with him a mallet, one of them meat mallets, got it from the kitchen. Anyway, there he was, smashing that emerald necklace—"

"Ruby," Mrs. Rostov said.

"—just *bashing* that thing, when old Mercer showed up and caught him."

"He *did?*"

"Yep. Caught him. Young Howard sittin' there on the floor, smilin' at the old man."

"Smiling?"

"Big row, big family row. The old man was for taking that young pup right down to the police station and handing him over right then and there. But his wife, Mrs. Mercer, and young Susan, they stopped him. Near had to tie him down, but they stopped him."

"Why?"

"The family *name,* young feller, the family *name!* Don't forget, now, the Scottwoods were pillars of the community. Churchgoers, town do-gooders, big mucky-mucks in all the organizations. People knew the Scottwood name clear up to Boston. That was very important to them. Family name's still important to lots of folks. You don't taint the family name, no siree. No sir!"

Nathan blinked.

"Howard, he hated the old man, and you couldn't right blame him, neither. They were both mean, both of them. Old Mercer, he used to whip the boy if ever he did anything wrong, and I mean whip him good. You know that old outbuilding where you and your young friend've been playing ball? Well, that's where young Howard received his whippings, with his grandfather's buggy whip. I never knew if Howard really wanted that money and jewelry or if he was just getting back at his grandfather. Hard to feel sorry for either one of them, you ask me."

"So . . . you think Mr. Mercer Scottwood haunts the porch, waiting for Howard to come back."

Mrs. Rostov shook her head, pursed her lips, and pulled on her needlepoint.

"That's what I think, son," Mr. Ainsley answered.

"But—but Howard's all grown up now."

"Ghosts don't know about growing up," Mr. Ainsley said. "They just remember what they remember. Years don't go by for ghosts, they just stay there. In their own time. You get a young boy out on that porch, old Mercer's going to try to fix his wagon!" Mr. Ainsley bonked his cane on the floor.

"Horsefeathers!" Mrs. Rostov said with a sniff.

"You think so? You think so, Rose? I know you better, but if you think it's horsefeathers, then you just come up there with the boy and me. You just come up there and you watch!"

"I'll do no such thing, Edward Ainsley, and don't you encourage such shenanigans either!"

"I will if I want to!" Mr. Ainsley said loudly, and shook his cane at her.

Mrs. Rostov ignored the outburst and leaned over toward Nathan. "Now, Nathan, you forget this nonsense," she said, "and don't pay any attention to this old coot! I never saw any such thing up there on that porch! If old Mercer only appears to children, then that's why Edward saw him, because he's just a little boy himself, even if he is past ninety!"

"Aha, you hear that, Nathan?" Mr. Ainsley barked. "She *knows* he's there! So, it's just for the boys, is it? Then just the boys will go. You go and get your friend and we'll go up there, the three of us! And you'll see something you'll never forget!" He poked Nathan's ankle with his cane.

"Now?" Nathan asked. "You mean now?"

"You can't go now," Mrs. Rostov said, turning to Mr. Ainsley. "Today we managed to get a doctor from town to come over to give you some tests."

"What tests?" Mr. Ainsley snapped.

"You can't remember anything. Honestly! *Blood pressure* test and all that."

"Oh, for heaven's sake." Mr. Ainsley waved his arm at her. "He can examine *you* instead! Or tell him to come another day."

Mrs. Rostov ignored him. "Not now, dear," she said to Nathan. "We can't have the doctor waste his visit."

"When the doctor leaves," Mr. Ainsley said. "*Then* we'll go."

"Okay," Nathan said. "Mr. Ainsley?"

"Eh?"

"How do you *know*? I mean, how do you know all that? About the Scottwoods?"

"Oh, I have firsthand knowledge, son. Firsthand knowledge, that's all I'll say about that." He chuckled to himself. "So you look out for me, son, I'll be there right after that doctor climbs into his buggy and rolls away."

"After *lunch!*" Mrs. Rostov snapped.

"The woman won't let me *be!*" Mr. Ainsley cried to the ceiling. "After lunch! You look out for me, son!"

"I will."

"And don't tell Susan anything about it, hear?"

Mrs. Rostov waved her needlepoint at him. "The boy's sister is not *Susan*, she's *Lucy!*"

Mr. Ainsley leaned forward and winked at Nathan.

The rain was heavy by noon. The guests stayed close to the inn, none of them caring to venture out. Henry brought his radio into the living room and

kept it tuned to the news and weather station. Cousin
Joan held an aerobics class in the rec room. Ten
people showed up for it, and they moved the Ping-
Pong and jigsaw tables off to one side.

"This is wonderful," Sandy whispered to Red. "I
told you it was a good idea. I'll bet they'll stay for a
book discussion right after she's through, what do
you think?"

"I think," Red said, "that these are the best
activities an inn could have if it's expecting a hurricane to hit at any moment."

"Oh, you," Sandy said.

Henry appeared on the stairs, carrying his radio. "Hey," he said nervously, "listen to this."

Everyone stopped moving, talking, and exercising. Joan turned off the music.

". . . into a severe thunderstorm," the announcer
was saying, "with high winds and rising tides. The
weather center is predicting the worst storm in ten
summers."

Karen, who had been maneuvered into the aerobics class by her distraught mother, threw her arms
into the air. "Oh, great!" she cried. "Just great!"

"Karen, please," her mother said.

Joan approached Sandy and Red. "I think it
would be a good idea to shutter the windows, don't
you?" she suggested tentatively.

Sandy and Red looked at each other. "Oh," Red
said, "sure. I guess so."

Joan turned around to face the group in the rec
room. "Excuse me, everybody, but we need some
volunteers to help shutter the windows. It's supposed to get really bad and we want to be prepared,"
she announced. "Is anyone willing?"

"Sure, I'll help," Donald said. He was behind
Henry on the stairs. "Where are the ladders?"

"They're in the storeroom next to the pantry,"

Joan said. "And I saw a big one out in the shed at the other end of the lawn out back. I noticed some old slickers in the chest on the back porch, so let's use them."

The guests began to move up the stairs, with Red in the lead.

"Joan—" Sandy said, giving her a hug.

"Shh, listen," Joan said, tilting her head. "That wind's getting bad. Let's go."

Chapter Thirteen

Lucy was out on the front porch working on the shutters when the sound of an old car engine made her turn. Her heart leapt as she recognized Chip's car pulling up to the curb.

Caroline and Chip came up the walk.

"The boutique is closed!" Caroline called against the wind. "Everyone is afraid of the height of the waves!" She was holding a raincoat over her head and the wind was whipping it back and forth as she jumped to get under the ceiling of the porch. "We came over to see if we could help you folks out!" She shook out her damp hair. "Our family is used to this—or sort of. How you doing?"

"Well, gee, that's so nice," Lucy said. "Hi, Chip. . . ."

"Hi—hey, let me do that, you'll never get that thing unhooked." He took Lucy's place in front of the window and began loosening the big shutter. "How about the others?" he asked as he worked.

"My father and some guests are helping with them."

"You should see the tide building," Caroline said. "It's scary!"

"Come on in—it's cold and wet out here," Lucy said.

Lucy thought that the big rooms seemed dark and frightening with the shutters closed. Everyone seemed to want to stay together, wandering in and out of the main parlor. Lunch was served by the few staff who'd arrived, and by Lucy and Caroline. Cousin Joan bustled off to check windows. Nathan and Ted sat on the stairs watching Mr. Ainsley who, in turn, was being watched by Mrs. Rostov.

"She won't let him do it, I bet," Nathan whispered to Ted.

Ted wrinkled his nose. He'd begun to think that Nathan was weird when he'd been dragged onto the screen-porch while the maid was cleaning. Then Nathan explained about the ghost and he really thought Nathan was weird. But there was no one else around to play with, and even if Nathan was crazy, he seemed nice and hanging out with him was more fun than hanging out with Karen or his parents.

"There's no such thing as ghosts," Ted said for the hundredth time to Nathan.

"I'll prove it to you," Nathan said earnestly, "if we can just get Mr. Ainsley away from Mrs. Rostov for a few minutes."

Ted nodded and scratched his ear. "We'll see."

Lucy ran to grab the ringing phone behind the front desk.

"Hello? *Hello?* Grandma? Can you hear me?" Lucy shouted, cupping her hand over the receiver.

"Yes, dear, but barely," Grandma answered. "There's static on the line."

"I know. We're having an awful storm. They say it's the worst in ten years. Maybe a hurricane."

"Listen to that wind!" Caroline was at Lucy's elbow. "I can't remember wind like that."

"Lucy? I just heard the weather report. You're supposed to get terrible rainstorms. Are you there?"

"I'm here, Grandma—"

"I'm getting worried, Lucy, I don't like this. How protected are you there? Where's your mother? Are all of you all right?"

"Yes, we're all okay, Grandma, honest, we just—"

"Where's your mother, Lucy? Are you sure that house is safe?"

As if on cue, a great crash was heard upstairs and several people screamed.

"Grandma, I have to hang up now, something's happened and I—"

"What? What happened?"

"I'm not sure yet, but don't worry, we're all fine. I'll call you back later."

"Lucy, don't go yet, what—"

"I *have* to, Grandma. I'll call you back, I promise!" She hung up, grabbed Caroline's arm, and together they raced up the stairs. The rain was pouring down through a gaping hole in the roof right over a small terrace and part of the hall on the third floor. Sandy stood there with Joan, Henry, Donald, and Chip.

"I can't believe this," Sandy cried, and burst into tears.

"Oh, Mom, don't cry. Mom—" Lucy went over to her mother and they hugged each other. "It'll be okay. Don't worry, Mom, we'll do something." She looked around the hallway.

"Right," said Joan. "Here's what we'll do! Chip! Donald! Henry!" She barked at them the way an army sergeant would, and they came forward like soldiers. "The hole's not that big." Joan screamed over the wind. "We can cover it with boat tarp. But we'll have to throw it over the top and ground the four corners. There's plastic tarp in the shed— let's move it!" The boys were already running down the stairs, nearly knocking Red over on his way up.

Joan pushed past him on her way down. "It was lightning, Red!" she yelled back over her shoulder. "But don't worry, we can tie two corners of the tarp on the balcony railing." She kept running and Red had to follow her partway down. "We can throw the whole thing over the roof corner and tie the other two sides from the ground! But we need a lot of rope. Look for rope!" And she was gone.

Red glanced at Sandy for only a moment before he took off to help.

"Oh, Lucy." Her mother was wiping her eyes.

"It'll be fine, Mom, you'll see."

By three o'clock the storm was raging even more wildly. Joan, assisted by Red and the three older boys, as well as Ted's father, had managed to cover the hole in the roof with tarpaulin. Joan's plan to anchor the two ends of the tarp to the ground by rope through its eyelets actually worked. With the hole temporarily sealed, Sandy and Lucy worked to mop up the wet mess in the hallway. They were wringing out rags when all the electricity went out.

"Oh, no!" Sandy cried. "This is just—I mean, how much are we supposed to—Oh, *damn*!" She smacked her hand against the wall.

"Mom? Slap your hand against the wall again so I can tell where you are!"

In spite of herself, Sandy smiled. "I'm here, Luce," she called.

"Okay. I'm coming toward you. We'll hold hands and feel our way along the wall till we get to the stairs. Okay, Mom?" She reached Sandy and grabbed her hand. "Come on, you can get it together, Mrs. Wall-Street-Mover-and-Shaker-Turned-Innkeeper!"

Sandy sniffed. "I guess I seem to be falling apart, here," she said in a little voice.

"Nah!"

"Are you scared?"

"No, are you?" said Lucy, trying to be brave.
She squeezed her mother's hand.

"No."

They both laughed.

"Mr. Ainsley?" Nathan hissed, tugging at the
old man's jacket. "How 'bout now?"

"Now's good," Mr. Ainsley whispered back. "If
I can get off this couch without my babysitter
noticing . . ." Nathan knew he meant Mrs. Rostov,
who was right next to him, with her hand over
his.

"But there're no lights," Ted said, crouching
down next to them. "How can you walk upstairs
with no lights, Mr. Ainsley?"

Mr. Ainsley chuckled and leaned over toward
the two boys. "Son, I've been going up and down
those stairs for more years than anyone else on this
earth, and I could do it if I were blind, which I'm
not. So you just think of a way to get this lady next
to me out of the way and we're off to the porch!"

Nathan scrunched up closer to Ted. "Okay, listen," he said. "I'm going to step over in front of the
couch and start talking to Mrs. Rostov. While I'm
doing that, you help get Mr. Ainsley up on his feet
and head for the stairs. I'll meet you on the way up
as soon as I know you're on your way, okay?"

"Okay," Ted said warily, "but I still think you're
nuts, Nathan."

"Where do you keep your candles?" Chip asked
Lucy.

Even in the middle of the crisis, she could hardly

answer. It seemed like the longest sentence Chip had ever spoken directly to her.

"Uh—" she managed, and cleared her throat. "There are some candles and kerosene lamps in the basement. On the shelves under the stairs. I'll—I'll show you."

"Good, come on," he said, and took her hand. She felt weak in the knees.

"Where's Caroline?" Chip asked as they made their way down the cellar stairs. "She wasn't with you upstairs, was she?"

"No, she was in the kitchen," Lucy answered. "I think Karen was with her."

Chip chuckled. "What's with Karen, anyway? She's like a prima donna. Did she ever do any kind of work in her life?"

"I don't think so," Lucy answered, and she felt an enormous weight lifting. I should have realized Karen is not his type, she thought. It doesn't matter *how* pretty she is.

"Lucy!" Chip cried suddenly.

"What? What?" She clutched at his hand tighter.

"Don't take another step. It's flooded down here!" He leaned against her, pushing her back up the stairs.

"Flooded?" she asked weakly.

"Yeah, it's—wait a minute. Jeez, it's about two feet."

"Two feet?"

"Maybe more. Hey! You got a backup generator? Sure, you must have! Let's go back up and ask your father. Come on!" He began to pull her.

"What'll we do?" she asked.

"The backup generator will start the sump pump. To pump out the basement. The electricity's off— the pump can't work. Come on, Lucy."

But she let go of his hand. "No, you go. I'll take

off my shoes and wade through for the candles and lamps."

"You sure?"

"Sure. I'll be right up. I can swim!" She leaned against the railing and watched him bound back up the stairs. He called me by name, she thought with a little sigh. Twice!

Chip moved through the big living room slowly. His eyes had become accustomed to the dark, but it was still hard to make out just who was who in the crowd of people.

"Mr. Weber?" he called as he stepped over this and around that. "Mr. Weber? Mr. *Weber*?"

"Is that you, Chip? It's Joan."

"Oh, good. Joan. The basement's flooded out. We need—"

"We need to get the generator going," she said. "It's on the side of the house. Red's getting flashlights."

"Lucy's getting candles and lamps."

"Fine. Well, as soon as one of them shows up, we'll go out there and get it started."

"We're here," Nathan breathed.

"I know, I know," Mr. Ainsley said. "Are you boys ready?"

"Ready," Nathan answered. "Are you okay, Ted?"

"Oh, sure, I'm fine."

"All right, then." Mr. Ainsley reached out and opened the door. "Let's go in."

Henry opened a drawer. "I think there're some batteries in here, Dad," he said.

"What kind?"

"Uh—" Henry felt around the inside of the drawer. "Little ones."

"We need D-cell. Anything else in there?"

"Ummm, I don't think so. Wait! Here they are." He pulled out a cardboard package holding two large batteries.

"Good boy," his father said. "But we could use some more. Donald, you there?"

"Uh-huh."

"Well, start opening drawers and feel around. I know we've got more batteries around here some-where."

Just then, Joan poked her head in the doorway. "Red?" she called.

"Yeah? Joan?"

"Yes. Lucy's got some kerosene lamps here."

"Oh, great."

"Here's one for you." She lit a match and held it to the wick. "It's about half filled. The other one's full and should last. I'm taking it out to read the instructions for the generator. Donald, come on out with Chip and me. We might need an extra hand."

"Okay."

"Edward? *Edward?*" Mrs. Rostov sat up, fright-ened. "Edward, where are you?" She reached out with her left hand and bumped someone.

"I'm not Edward," a young voice answered. "I'm Karen."

"Karen? What happened to the gentleman who was sitting here a moment ago? I must have dozed off. . . ." Her hands began to flutter.

"He left, so I sat down," Karen answered. "There's no place to sit around here."

"He left? Oh, my."

"It's okay, he was with my brother and Lucy's

brother. They probably took him to the bathroom or something."

Mrs. Rostov covered her mouth with her fingers. "Oh, dear, I don't think that's where they went. Oh, *dear*."

"Don't worry, now," Karen said. "I'm sure they're all right."

Mrs. Rostov reached for Karen's hands. "I do worry about that man. I've known him for so long. . . ."

"Isn't he your husband?" Karen asked.

"Oh, my, no, we're just old friends. I come here for a month every year. I have since I was a girl and used to come with my parents. Edward's been living here year round. He worked on the boats until he retired." She clucked her tongue. "Old coot, he doesn't know what he's doing, wandering around this place in the dark. Honestly, you've got to watch him like a baby. I swear, if something happens to him . . ."

"Nothing will happen," Karen said gently. "The boys will bring him right back here."

"You're a sweet girl," Mrs. Rostov said, and reached to touch Karen's cheek.

"Me?" Karen couldn't remember a time when anyone called her sweet.

"Yes. I can't really see your face too well, but I can tell you're a lovely young girl. Pretty, too, I'm sure."

Karen felt herself blush.

"Lucy Weber's a lovely girl, too," Mrs. Rostov said. "It's about time the young people in this place were nice. The last set of children who grew up here put seashells in the beds!"

Karen giggled.

"They did, and sand too. And they put salt in the sugar bowls!"

Karen didn't mention she had done things just like that at overnight camp.

"But every now and then," Mrs. Rostov went on, "we find young people like you and Lucy and Nathan . . . thoughtful children with good manners. Then it's a pleasure to think about the next generations."

Karen swallowed.

"What did you say your name was, dear?" Mrs. Rostov asked.

"Karen Jordan."

"Such a pretty name. Karen, will you do something for me?" Mrs. Rostov groped for the girl's hands and took them in her own. "Would you mind . . . just staying with me? Until Edward comes back? I'd rather not be sitting here alone. I just feel—"

"Yes. Sure. Of course, I'll sit here," Karen said. "As long as you want." The woman actually thought she was *sweet*!

They didn't close the door, but just stepped inside—the three of them—Mr. Ainsley, flanked on either side by Ted and Nathan. Wordlessly, they moved together to the right and stood against the wall.

"You okay, Mr. Ainsley?" Nathan asked.

"Never better!" Mr. Ainsley boomed.

Nathan gripped his arm tighter.

"What's supposed to happen, anyway?" Ted asked. "I feel stupid."

"Shh!" Nathan said. "Just stand here and listen."

"Listen to what, the wind? This is weird, Nathan—"

They all suddenly had an eerie sensation as if something had bumped against the wall. Chills ran up Nathan's spine. He dug his fingers so hard into

Mr. Ainsley's arm that the old man reached to loosen them.

"It's all right, Nathan, it's all right," the old man murmured.

"Boy!" a voice said.

Nathan's ears tingled. *"Did you hear? Did you hear?"* he asked.

"Yeah, you said 'Boy,' " Ted answered.

"*I* didn't say it."

"Boy!" the voice said again.

"That you, Mercer?" Mr. Ainsley croaked. "Speak up, we can hardly hear you!" He sounded brave, but Nathan could feel his arm tremble.

Another bump, this one harder and louder, shook the wall.

"Boy!" the voice cried.

Ted whimpered. "I want to go back," he said. "Come on, Nathan, this isn't funny."

"You heard it, right?" Nathan said, his fear momentarily forgotten in his delight at having been believed.

"I wanna go back," Ted wailed. The porch felt ice-cold.

"Mercer, you listen to me, now," Mr. Ainsley croaked. "These are good boys! They are not Howard. Howard's all grown up! You're not going to do anything to Howard on this porch. You're waiting around this porch for nothing. You're depriving the inn of business. Let the guests get some good fun out here! Now, go get yourself some rest and leave these folks alone, you hear? *You hear me, Mercer Scottwood?"* This last was yelled, as loud as a gentleman over ninety could yell, and to accompany his request, he banged his cane on the floor.

A whoosh of icy wind swept through the porch. Mr. Ainsley's straw boater was knocked from his head as Nathan's hair stood up on end and Ted's, which was longer, whipped across his cheeks.

The icy wind seemed to circle them, even though their backs were pressed tight against the wall and they held on to each other with all of their might. Then suddenly the icy wind stopped.

It just stopped.

They felt the ordinary dampness of the porch. The iciness had disappeared.

No one spoke. All three were breathing rapidly.

Mr. Ainsley broke the silence by coughing.

"Oh, gee—Mr. Ainsley—" Nathan turned to support him better.

"No, no, it's all right." Mr. Ainsley cleared his throat again. "You okay there, son?" He meant Ted, whose shoulder he patted.

"Uh . . . I guess. What *happened*?"

"What happened! I dropped my hat is what happened. Pick it up for me, will you?"

Ted groped, found it, and handed it to the old man.

"Thanks. He's gone," Mr. Ainsley said.

"He is?" Nathan's voice quavered.

"Certainly he is! Can't you feel it? Can't you?"

"Um . . . well . . . the cold's gone."

"The cold's gone. Mercer took it with him. Just needed someone to tell him he didn't need to be here anymore."

"What do you mean?" Nathan asked. "He never needed to be here."

"Funny thing about ghosts, Nathan. They're stubborn. They hang around the place where something happened that bothered them. They hang around, and they hang around . . . They don't even know it's a long time later and new people are around—*live* people." Mr. Ainsley chuckled to himself. "And if any of those live people see them, why,

those people are just scared right out of their wits,
see? Well, not you and me, of course, but others, I
mean. So what the live people have to do, see, is
they have to say right out loud: 'Go 'way, ghost! It's
time for you to pass on! No one here for you to be
mad at anymore! Everyone's gone on, now you go,
too! Shoo, scat!' See?"

"And that's all?"

Mr. Ainsley shrugged. "That's all. Pretty simple.
You just have to explain to 'em. Don't you like having things explained?"

"Well, yeah. . . ."

"Sure, you do. Once something's explained, it
don't bother you no more."

"Will someone please explain to *me* just what
happened, anyway?" Ted said finally.

"Well, sure," Mr. Ainsley said. "Nathan, is that
old wicker couch still out here?"

"It's still there, Mr. Ainsley."

"All right, then. Rose will probably be frettin',
but she can just wait. Let me go sit down on it and
I'll tell you. See, son, old Mercer Scottwood had a
grandson name of Howard, who was pretty mean.
And one day, he . . ."

Chip held the lamp higher. "Can you read it
now?" he asked.

Joan squinted her eyes. "Yes . . . yes, I can see
it. Okay. First, check the gas in the generator." She
waited while Chip used the light to do it. "Okay?"

"Yeah, okay. Here's the light back. What's next?"

"Well, we have to shut off one switch so we can
throw the other one to power the house. We want all
the power going into the house. Now let's see where
that electrical box is. . . ."

Chip moved the lamp around.

"There!" Donald pointed. "It's over there, Miss, uh—"

"Joan. You can just call me Joan, Donald."

"Gee, Joan, where'd you learn how to do all this stuff?"

"What stuff? There, the switch is off. Let's see what's next."

"All this mechanical stuff!" Donald cried.

"Oh." Joan stopped and looked at him. "Oh, that. Well . . . my husband, Harry—" She stopped, swallowed. "He's not around anymore, but he never brought home much money, and I didn't either, so we just couldn't afford to pay someone to fix things."

"Yeah, so you learned how to do it yourself?"

"I had to, I guess. I took a night school course."

"Well, you must've liked it. You learned important stuff that's useful. At school."

"Hold that lamp nearer, Chip," Joan said. "It wasn't so much that I liked it a whole lot, Donald." She squinted her eyes at the instruction sheet. "It's just—I needed to know it. And then I got to like it, I guess, because I was proud of myself for learning new stuff. Okay, it says here, 'Pull out choke in small, short jerks. Then slowly push in choke.' "

"Did it," Chip said. The generator fired up.

"*Yayyy!*" Joan and Chip cheered together and slapped palms.

"You mean you learned a whole lot of stuff you weren't even interested in, huh?" Donald asked. He'd forgotten the generator and why they were there.

"Yes . . . but I got interested in it. Listen, Donald, you always use what you learn. Maybe not right away, but learning's never wasted. The more you learn, the more prepared you are for anything. I never knew I'd need to know how to fix a hole in a roof. Come on, guys, let's go back and make sure everything's working."

"Joan?" Donald tugged at her slicker. "How come your husband's not around anymore?"

Joan looked at him and didn't answer.

"Because he's nuts not to want to be here with you. He's really crazy."

Joan bit her lip and pushed him ahead of her out into the rain.

Chapter Fourteen

As the light burst on in the big living room, the guests cheered and clapped.

Sandy, Lucy, and Caroline formed a three-way hug. From her vantage point Lucy noticed Mrs. Rostov patting Karen's hand and smiling.

"Wow," Caroline said. "I guess Karen was useful after all."

Nathan, Mr. Ainsley, and Ted worked their way down the stairs. Mr. Ainsley seemed bouncier than he had in a long time.

"Edward!" Mrs. Rostov cried, jumping to her feet. "Where have you been?"

"Sit down, Rose. Stop fussing!" Mr. Ainsley said, waving his fingers impatiently. "I've been evicting an unwanted individual, that's all."

When Joan came in, dripping wet, along with Donald and Chip, they received a round of cheers. Sandy hurried over.

"I can't believe you!" Sandy said, wrapping her arms around her wet cousin. "Where did you learn how to do all those things? You're marvelous! Why didn't you say anything?"

Joan looked blank. "It never occurred to me," she said. "We hadn't had any problems until now."

"Well, you're hired full-time and forever as of this minute!" Red said, as he and Henry joined them. "You're our new handyman! We hope you'll say yes."

"Handy*woman*," Sandy said.

"Handy*person!*" Chip added. He saw his sister standing with Lucy and went over to join them.

"Nice work, Chipper," Caroline said. "But you're all wet."

"So I'm all wet! Does that mean I don't get a hug? Everyone's getting hugged," he complained.

"Eeeyew, not me," Caroline said. "Lucy'll hug you instead. She's wet, too. Go on, hug him, Lucy." She pushed them together. Lucy didn't know whether to kill Caroline or kiss her.

"Hi."

They all turned. Karen had joined them. "Thought it was time to be with a younger crowd," she said.

Lucy was the first to speak. "Thanks for staying with Mrs. Rostov," she said.

"She was nice," Karen said, but she was looking directly at Chip as she spoke.

"Well!" Caroline said. "It looks as though the wind has died down."

"Yeah, I think the storm's on the way out." Chip turned to Lucy. "You'll have to get someone for that roof pretty soon," he said. "Captain Andy has two sons who could fix it. And I could help."

"Great."

"Anybody hungry?"

Caroline laughed. "That means *you* are. Come on, Lucy, let's see what's in the kitchen. You want to help, Karen?"

"I think I'll stay here for a little while," she said as she stared at Chip.

"Suit yourself," Caroline called. "Come on, Chipper, you don't think you're getting waited on, do you?"

Chip laughed. "Not by you, for sure!" he said, and followed the girls into the kitchen, leaving Karen staring after him.

*   *   *

"Okay, you saw it, right?" Nathan said to Ted as the two were wolfing potato chips in the dining room.

"Saw what? I didn't see anything," Ted said.

"Come on, Ted. You did too!"

"I *heard* something. But I'm still not sure what it was I heard."

"I brought you there for proof!" Nathan said. "I wasn't imagining I heard anything on that porch, was I? Well, was I?"

Ted said, "Can we play basketball in your basement?"

"No! Come on, Ted, tell me you heard what I heard!"

Ted wiped salt from his mouth with the back of his hand. "Look, Nathan," he said, "there's a big storm out there. There were no lights and a lot of scared people moving around this place. Mr. Ainsley's nice, but he's a thousand years old, and when you get that old you hear things. There were noises and stuff, sure, but I don't know what they were and neither do you, okay?"

Nathan wrinkled his nose. "So what does that mean?" he asked.

"It means I sure wish the storm would quit and everything would dry up so we could go shoot some hoops!"

The storm was just about over by six o'clock. Sandy and the girls managed to get some chicken fried, potatoes baked, and a big salad tossed. Donald's father had made his bread delivery that morning, so there was even fresh bread on hand. They set up a buffet in the dining room and had a delicious evening meal.

Henry noticed Donald's eyes were wandering around the room. "Hey," he said, sidling up to Donald. "I know who you're looking for."

"Oh, yeah? Who?"

"My sister, that's who," Henry teased. "I know you have a thing for my ugly sister. You've been watching her all summer!"

"No," Donald said, and gestured with his chicken leg. "Your sister's right over there."

"Then who is it?"

"No one," Donald said. But now he was craning his neck to better scan the room.

"No, right, you're not looking for anyone," Henry said. "You're doing aerobics with your neck. I'm gonna get some more food."

"Yeah," Donald said, almost to himself. "Aerobics . . ." He put down his plate and hurried over to where he had seen her come in from the basement door.

"Hi, Joan!" he said, grinning at her. "Hey, you want me to get you a plate of food? Or something?"

Lucy and her father stood together beneath the covered hole in the roof on the third floor.

"Some mess, huh?" Lucy said, giving her father a half smile. She was still wearing her patched jeans, dry now from the storm. Her hair lay in matted clumps, but her face managed to look shiny and scrubbed.

"Uh-*huh*," Red said, and smiled back. His face was dirty and sooty. "Some mess."

"Do you think you're going to stick it out, Dad?" Lucy asked. "Mom was pretty scared back there."

"I know. I was, too, to be honest. There's a lot more to running an inn than either of us ever imagined. We'll stick it out, all right. Truth is, we like it. And Cousin Joan turned out to be better than a fat Christmas bonus! She wants to stay, and we want her to." Red paused and studied his daughter. "How about you?"

Suddenly Henry and Sandy appeared at the top of the stairs. Henry was already in his pajamas. He was carrying a glass of milk and a book.

" 'Night, Dad," he said, ignoring Lucy. "It was fun today."

"Yeah." Red laughed. "It was a ball."

"No, I mean it. It could have been serious, but no one got hurt and we had fun."

"You know, Henry," Red said, "you have one of those storms out at sea, it's not so much fun."

"Yeah." Henry looked down at his bare feet. "I guess I'll have to put off going to sea. For a while, anyway."

"You changed your mind?"

"Oh, no. I didn't change my mind. I still think it would be a great idea. It was Donald. He changed his."

"Donald?"

"Yeah. He's staying in school."

"Really?"

"Yeah. He says it was his idea, but I think it was his parents'. I mean, I can't see his parents really letting him quit. He's just trying to big-man it, saying it's his idea. Donald never liked school. Don'tcha think so, Dad?"

Red shrugged. "You never know," he said.

"Nah. It was his parents. 'Night, Dad."

"Good night, Henry."

"G'*night,* Henry," Lucy said to his back.

"Oh. Yeah, g'night, Lucy."

They all watched him disappear down the stairs.

"Well," Sandy said. "One problem solved for the moment." She turned to her husband and daughter. "You two looked like you were engaged in a serious discussion, there. Did we interrupt something?"

"I'd just asked Lucy if she had decided yet what she's going to do when the summer is over."

"Ohh. And the answer is?"

Lucy looked from her mother to her father. It was in that moment that she knew that although her answer was the one she had known it would be, now her reason was different. She just hadn't put it into words, even for herself. She *had* kept the open mind she'd promised her parents she'd keep.

"I want to go back," she said. "To live with Grandma. To school. To the city." She saw her mother's face crumble.

"I really thought you'd begun to like it here," Red said. Lucy could see the hurt in his eyes. "I thought we'd won you over after all."

"You don't understand!" Lucy cried. "I *do* like it here, *I love it*! And if it's all right and we can afford it, I want to be able to come back for weekends and vacations."

Sandy was shaking her head. "I don't understand, Lucy. Does it have to do with Chip?"

"Oh, no, Mom!" She laughed. "It sure would have been nice if he was interested in me, but honest—it doesn't have anything to do with Chip.

"I love you and I love the Scottwood. It's just that I don't think I'm ready to live here year round, isolated this way. I don't think I'm ready to ride a school bus every day with a small group of people who've known each other since kindergarten. That'll be fine for Henry and Nathan, but I'm fifteen and in tenth grade and I miss my friends. I want to hear about Canada by bike and about all the college summer programs and about all the new people everyone met. And I want to tell them about the new people *I* met.

"Look, maybe I'll hate it, maybe living with Grandma will be hard. But you were the ones who told me I had a choice, and that means you love me enough to let me try. And if it doesn't work . . . you won't rent my room, right?" She tried a smile.

"Lucy—" Sandy glanced at Red, "I know we gave you the choice, but—"

Lucy's face darkened. "You're taking it back?" she asked. "My right to choose?"

"Luce, wait a minute," Red said. "When you talk about rights—"

Lucy interrupted him. "No, Daddy, I know what you're going to say, and you're right. I tried my best this summer, I worked real hard, but I know that running the inn wasn't on my shoulders, it was on yours. So we're not equal. I'm glad you pay the bills. But you still made a bargain, you still promised!"

"We're not going back on our bargain," Red said firmly, and Sandy looked at him. "No, we won't, Sandy. Although we could. We're your parents, Lucy, and we can say we've changed our minds. You know that, don't you?"

"I know that," Lucy said defiantly, "but if you did that I'd never trust you again. I wouldn't respect you anymore."

"That's why we won't do it. You've always been able to trust us, and we don't want to change that. And besides, you deserve your choice. You did work hard. And I think you did keep an open mind."

Sandy sighed. "I guess," she said, "that we didn't really think you'd make the choice you have made. I guess that was it, honey. Oh, Lucy, I never thought you'd want to leave here—leave us."

"I love you both for letting me do this," Lucy said. "I'm really not leaving you. You're just letting me grow up."

"I just couldn't picture you living with Grandma. She'll stay on your back, you know. Look, she still hasn't really let go of *me* all these years. But we can't stop you from growing up. And as for Grandma, you'll find out for yourself!"

"Grandma! I just remembered." Lucy slapped her forehead with an open palm. "I forgot to call her back! Oh, Mom, she called when the storm broke and I promised I'd—"

"I'll do it." Sandy leaned forward to kiss her daughter's cheek. "I'll call her," she said. "We have a lot to talk about."

About the Author

JUDIE ANGELL lives in South Salem, New York, with her husband, a musician, and their two sons. She is the author of many books for young adults, including *Dear Lola, A Word From Our Sponsor, Secret Selves, One Way to Ansonia,* and the Bantam Starfire novel *Leave the Cooking to Me.*